A Twin Room

JON NEAL

Copyright © 2022 Halcyon Enterprises Ltd
All rights reserved.
ISBN: 9798785063228

Dedicated to Justin.
Of course.

1.

It had been one hundred and eighty-five days.
A lifetime. And yet fleeting.

'The forecast is uncertain,' I said, glancing up at the overcast sky. 'We'll have to pack for every eventuality.'

From the bedroom window, I looked at the familiar streetscape lined with trees and parked cars. Curtains were drawn. Only the cat from number thirty-eight prowled territorially along the pavement. A blackbird serenaded the new morning.

I returned to the piles of clothes on the bed. Definitely in danger of packing too many things.

'It's not as if we're going for long. Or abroad,' I said. 'There'll be shops if we need to pick up anything we've forgotten.'

In my mind's eye I pictured gift shops geared to tourists festooned with fishing nets, beachballs, and bright coloured buckets and spades. And sweet shops stacked with candy-striped rock. We had never thought whether there were practical shops like supermarkets.

I tried not to let my mind wander. Better to focus on the task at hand.

'It's an adventure,' I said, trying not to notice how hollow my jolly tone sounded.

A tiny niggle of anxiety crept in. It peered over my shoulder.

Trying to suppress it I began to purposefully pack the small suitcase. I placed a layer and smoothed it before adding another, sensing immediately that it wasn't all going to fit in. With a dogged determination to prove myself wrong I shoved the remainder as hard as I could into each corner, pulled down the lid and struggled until the zip was entirely closed.

I eyeballed the bulging suitcase as if in some perverse Mexican stand-off with it. If it could speak, I wondered what it would have said to me.

The clock radio beside the bed confirmed that it was still early. But time was passing.

'We should avoid the traffic if we head off soon,' I said.

The house seemed particularly quiet, and I wondered whether it was sulking.

Yesterday I had let Charlotte next door know that there would be nobody home for a few days. She and Scott have two young girls. They have always been very friendly to us.

'Are you going somewhere nice?' she asked with a somewhat pitying expression upon her face. I explained the situation and she said she had wondered. Her two girls ran around her legs and shrieked. 'Of course we'll keep an eye on the place whilst you're away.'

As I walked back down their front path, a monumental tide of emotion swept up within me and I found that I could not look back to give her a wave. It was as if a tsunami of tears might overflow from my eyes and I found myself blinking them back in short heavy gulps. I remembered, somewhat randomly, playing with domino tiles as a boy. Lining them up in a long snaking line, then watching with delight as one topple brought the others down in a satisfying clatter. Closing the neighbours front gate, it felt as if the first domino had been pushed. In saying these things aloud they were becoming real. And like it or not, the other dominoes would inevitably tumble.

I struggled to lift the suitcase from the bed on my own. But with a decisive tug it relented and I manoeuvred it to the floor before dragging it noisily down the stairs where it sat disgruntled in the hallway by the front door. I was breathless. It took a moment to compose myself. Sometimes I forget that I'm not a young man anymore.

My heart was pounding and I felt a little dizzy. I grasped the end of the banister and focused on my breathing trying to avoid that peer over my shoulder again.

Having steadied myself, I gave the house a once over to check that all the taps were firmly turned off, windows closed and the back door locked. And then proceeded to go back and double-check them all again. 'You never can be too certain,' I said.

I decided to leave the curtains half-drawn which gave the place an eerie semi abandoned feel. Its frozen tidiness made it look like a stage set of a play. The lounge, in particular, seemed to be anticipating the arrival of characters to bring the place to life. And all the accumulated objects, from the artwork on the wall to the books on the shelves, had an air of mere artifice. Each of them potential props to be used in telling a story.

The clock on the mantelpiece ticked. I was surprised how little I had noticed its sound over all these years. It was the slow sound of dominoes falling, I thought glumly.

I gathered up my wallet, keys and mobile phone from the table in the hallway.

As satisfied as I could be that the house was secure, I opened the front door to the early morning and hefted the suitcase to our car on the driveway. There was a well-thumbed road atlas in the glove compartment, but I was confident that I would know the way. I had filled the old girl with a full tank of petrol the day before in readiness for the journey. As I stood at the churning pump, nozzle in hand, I couldn't remember the last time she'd had a really good run.

I glanced up at the façade of the semi-detached house as I opened the driver's door. I thought I could describe every single brick of it. And yet today it looked different, but I couldn't see in what way.

The car interior had a familiar comfortable aroma to it. Years of *us*, I supposed. The fabric on the seats had faded slightly. An old air freshener in the shape of a pine tree, purchased at a petrol station, hung from the rear-view mirror. Long passed its useful life.

I turned the key in the ignition and felt relieved that the engine turned over. It had been a reliable car. The date stamps in the service history logbook were testament to its regular care and upkeep.

In releasing the hand brake, I couldn't help thinking again about the taps and the windows and the doors. 'We did switch everything off, didn't we?'

For a moment, I was in danger of being stuck in a terrible paralysis. Neither being able to move forward or to go back – which, of course, is always impossible. I reprimanded myself for being unnecessarily fastidious. It was on the verge of becoming an unhealthy habit.

'We can do this,' I said. 'We *can* do this.'

With a gentle dab on the accelerator, the car edged down the driveway and down across the gutter onto the road itself. Having looked both ways twice to ensure that the way forward was clear, we were suddenly on our way. The journey had commenced without a last look back at the house. It had already gone from view. I could feel my heart racing. My fingers clutched the steering wheel tightly.

It was what we had talked about. And it was actually happening.

The initial passing streetscapes were fraught with memories of us doing things together. To have lived in an area for so long seemed to have almost engrained us in its very being. We had seen the changes, witnessed together the creep of the capital out towards us and ultimately consuming us into its metropolitan spread. The leafiness that had first attracted us had remained, but it had been transformed by new tower block developments, increasing traffic, and the constant overhead whine of aeroplanes.

On the high street, the lights on the pedestrian crossing outside the twenty-four-hour mini supermarket turned red. A white-haired woman wearing a camel coat and walking a small dog shuffled across. Determined not to look at the other shop frontages, I fixed my eyes on her. She acknowledged my patience with a quick nod and, I think, a surprised flicker of recognition.

Moving on, I fixed my sight ahead as if travelling through a tunnel. I was struck by the activity on the pavements in my peripheral vision. Lorries were unloading boxes from metal storage cages. People jogged and cycled. Postal workers were delivering. And a steady flow of commuters descended upon the entrance to the train station.

'So many people out for the early worms!' I said.

I navigated my way out of town with an unexpected degree of concentration. Driving was not something I'd practised regularly, and I was surprised to remember how much attention it required. The process of both being alert and simultaneously looking ahead felt particularly foreign to me. I heard a car horn blast. Whether it was at me, I couldn't say. Perhaps I had not given way correctly at a junction. Or maybe I was driving too slowly. Or fast.

My heart rate rose.

The landscape soon evolved into the nondescript terrain on the town's outskirts. The road was dotted with large square industrial units and it quickly expanded into multiple lanes. Whether by luck or instinct, I navigated into the correct flow on to a vast churning roundabout and joined – with another accompanying flurry of horns – the motorway.

I stuck to the slow lane as vehicles shot by me.

'Was it always this busy?' I asked, but my voice was drowned out by the ferocious rumble of an articulated truck passing by.

A few spots of rain hit the windscreen.

Anxiety was bubbling up again.

Thankfully, the weather did not deteriorate and soon we reached our junction which led on to a considerable stretch of dual carriageway on which the traffic seemed happy to whiz by me in the slow lane. I considered switching on the radio. But opted against it. Too much of a risk.

Who knew which of our songs they might be playing?

The city now lay far behind us. The vista opened up to vast fields. At one point the road wound down a hillside affording a panoramic outlook of towns and villages nestled amongst the countryside. I kept one eye on the road as I tried to take in the view.

I felt very small and insignificant as we settled into the journey.

The car wound its way through hedgerows and overhanging branches. The speed limit varied as we passed through villages with lonesome public houses and picturesque ponds.

The road signs, I noticed with some relief, were now displaying our destination. My memory had served me well.

My thumb tapped involuntarily on the steering wheel.

I cursed myself for thinking again about the taps and the windows and the doors. The house suddenly seemed so very far away.

The road rose steeply and the engine began to moan about it. I moved the car into a lower gear. We were slowing.

I'd once heard that a car journey is the ideal place to hold a non-confrontational conversation. To speak whilst not having to have eye contact. To have the distraction of driving or taking in the view.

As we reached the peak of the hill a board, partly obscured by overgrown shrubs, proclaimed 'Welcome to Somerton-on-Sea!'

The town and the grey sea lay beyond.

'Do you think we'll be happy here?' I asked.

But inevitably, there was no reply. And I dared not turn my head for fear of seeing the empty seat beside me.

2.

'Here for the festival?'

I fumbled in my wallet to try and give her the right change. 'The festival?'

She prodded her finger at the front page of the folded local newspaper I had placed on the counter. My nostrils twitched at the old-fashioned smell of ink on paper. 'Busiest week of the year.'

My heart sank.

'Hordes of tourists pile in,' she continued. 'Won't be able to move for the coaches. They have to open up one of the fields as an extra carpark.'

This wasn't what we had imagined at all. 'We're just visiting for a few days,' I said. Which wasn't exactly true on several counts.

The woman nodded her head. She had a friendly face but I wondered, a little unkindly, whether she might be a gossip. Her upright posture suggested someone who was long-established and confident in her domain. Here, amongst the shelves of magazines, sweets and scratch cards, she clearly ruled the roost.

'You'll never hear *me* complaining about the crowds mind. They're what keeps us afloat. Some of the faces return year after year.'

I found myself warming to her. 'Important to support the independent retailer,' I said, knowing too well myself the commitment required to keep a business running.

'Are you staying somewhere nice?'

'A guesthouse. Thought we'd make the most of the day before checking in this afternoon.'

'You were lucky to get a room.'

I couldn't recall them mentioning any of this to me during our telephone conversation. But with hindsight, I had been in a fog. I could hardly remember it at all. They had sounded distant and the things we'd said to one another felt disjointed. Had they said they'd been in rather a muddle? My preoccupied mind had been distracted. I hadn't listened. 'They were a little out of sorts,' I remember saying to you after the call. 'We must have caught them at an inconvenient time.'

'You should try and catch some of the events,' she said. 'There's a parade. And a fireworks display. All the dates and times are listed.' She was nudging again at the newspaper for which I had laid out coins for her.

I doubted whether there would be spare time. I was buying the newspaper for other reasons. I picked it up and propped it beneath my arm. During the early morning drive I had fretted that the plan had not been fully developed. We had only ever been excited about the bigger picture. And now reality was biting.

The newspaper was the first considered step.

I thanked her. First contact with the locals had been positive.

'Enjoy your stay,' she said. 'Hope to see you again soon.'

As I stepped on to the pavement, I had a strange sensation of slipping through my imagination into reality. Were we really there? It was a surreal moment of emerging from layers of memories and conversations.

At the door of the newsagent stood a rack of picture-perfect postcards of Somerton-on-Sea. On each of them the sun shone. There was blue sky. Everybody smiled. The garden beds on the promenade were bursting with blousy perennials.

The town was already beginning to show signs of preparing for the anticipated crowds. I looked at the palm trees, incongruent against the metallic grey sky. A mechanical street sweeping vehicle crept noisily along the gutter. Shutters lifted and doors unlocked on shops, which on first inspection appeared to be a mish-mash of charity shops and convenience stores. Seagulls, impossibly over-sized, perched upon any available ledge or streetlamp. Some tilted back their heads and cawed melancholic howls. Some swooped across the urban terrain. Others took the time to scavenge what they could from the bins.

Paintwork peeled from the building frontages. I noticed that some walls retained the painted ghost signs of industries resigned to history: tailors, bakers, greengrocers.

Small groups of people hung around the benches. Around them lay scattered detritus of bottles and beer cans. In one doorway a crumpled sleeping bag concealed a person beneath.

It was not how I'd remember it from when I'd holidayed here as a boy. I remembered it being bigger and softer at the edges. Like the postcards, it had been sunnier. But perhaps everything had looked bigger and sunnier back then. Hadn't the summers stretched on endlessly? Hadn't the horizons once looked limitless? All the promise of unexplored adventures ahead and untapped potential just waiting to be mined.

'Do you think it's changed?' I said. 'Or is it a case of rose-tinted spectacles?'

I was in danger of feeling overwhelmed. My heart banged and I felt dizzy again. The ground seemed to tilt beneath me.

I consciously steadied myself. It was early and I hadn't had breakfast. Things would look better after caffeine and something to eat.

My first appraisal of available eateries was not hopeful. They were all the cookie-cutter brand coffee shops that you detested. The type furnished with ubiquitous chrome, wood and burgundy décor. Prints on the wall of olive groves and young couples astride vespas on cobbled streets. 'They don't have any local charm or character. Sucking the lifeblood out of communities to line the pockets of a corporation.'

I was happy to hear your words. Your determination to stand up for what you believed in was what had first attracted me to you. You had always been as solid as a rock.

Refusing to give up, a meander away from the immediate town centre uncovered a small section of ramshackle enterprises that would meet your approval: a second-hand bookshop, an iron mongers, even a tiny art gallery. I noticed ahead a small number of tables and chairs – some already occupied - beneath a striped awning, indicating the type of place we hoped to find. The sky looked to have lightened slightly at this discovery. Its heavy gloom had lifted to a thinner layer of cloud which conveyed the tantalising promise that sunshine might eventually breakthrough.

I entered the café with the local newspaper still clutched in my hand and scanned for the perfect spot.

It had an eclectic mix of furniture. Wooden tables of various sizes accompanied by mismatched chairs – some of which were furnished by cushions in shades of purple, blue, oranges and yellow. A counter with an old-fashioned till displayed cakes and pastries beneath glass belljars. A waft of breakfasts being cooked hinted at a kitchen nearby.

A woman with an angular black bob haircut frothed milk industriously at a coffee machine. She greeted me efficiently above the hiss of the machine and indicated for me to take a seat.

The place was reassuringly clean.

A smattering of customers chatted to one another filling the space with a comfortable hum. Their easy familiarity with the surrounds gave off the impression of locals in their own environment. But the atmosphere was inclusive and there was no sense of being an outsider.

My shoulders relaxed. The sound of tinkling crockery and the al fresco whoops of gulls outside were more reminiscent of the Somerton-on-Sea we'd imagined.

A menu was propped against a small glass vase of wildflowers. The text on the card was littered with poor grammar and spelling mistakes which instantly enamoured me to it. A quick glance showed that a tantalising array of breakfast and lunch selections were available.

Having chosen my option, I flicked through the local newspaper to find the pertinent section. Whilst spreading the pages open and smoothing them out on the table a bulky shadow appeared beside me. For a disorientating instant I thought it was you. But an awkward second of me blinking my eyelids and composing myself revealed a stocky young man grinning at me. A blue apron was tied around his waist.

'You look to find a new home here?' he said with a thick accent I couldn't identify.

'Sorry?' I said, not comprehending.

'New home?' he said again, this time indicating towards the print on the table.

We both scanned the grainy photos of the property section before me. They looked nothing more than a blur of doors, windows and roofs. 'Yes,' I answered. 'We need to find a home. We *have* to.'

'*Have to* are strong words.'

'Indeed. They are. But an offer has been accepted on our house, so finding one is now a necessity.'

'It sounds like you have some urgency.'

I nodded.

He ran his hand contemplatively across his short-cropped hair. 'You are not from here?'

A surge of unease rose within me. Was I an imposter?

'No,' I said. 'But I used to have holidays here as a child.'

'I am not from here either. But it is a good place to come. I am from Poland. And once I knew nobody here. But now I am part of a whole community.' He grinned again. 'Do you know any person here?'

There was Lana and Pearl, of course. But for some reason I didn't know if they counted. 'I know a few,' I said.

'And now you know another. Now you know me - Wiktor.'

'My name is Munro.'

'Munro? That's an unusual name.'

'Yes. I'm actually Michael. Munro is my surname. But all my friends know me as Munro.'

'Then I will know you as Munro too.' He held out his big hand. I lifted mine and he grasped it warmly with both of his and shook enthusiastically.

'You want drink? You want food? You'll need strength for your house hunt.'

I told him what I wanted and before I knew it he'd left me to the blurry photos before me. I tried to focus on them individually but their lack of context made them slip and slide around in my vision. Did the future lie in one of these grainy pictures? It felt like a daunting prospect. Something rather momentous.

Shortly after this, the efficient woman with the angular bob appeared at my table and asked to take my order. A little confusion arose as we politely disagreed as to whether my order had already been placed. Amicably she took the details again and I placed the misunderstanding down to a hiccough in communication.

Back out on the street, the optimism I'd felt in the form of a mug of coffee and bacon sandwich soon evaporated. The accelerating bustle thrust me into a solitary muddle.

The discussions about relocating to Somerton-on-Sea suddenly felt nebulous. They'd been a fantasy, hadn't they? An escape from the day-to-day. A glimpse of a hopeful future. But looking back at them now, they'd never been about the practicalities of *how* we would do it.

Or when: *One day...*

Only then, staring despondently at the plate-glass window, were those practicalities apparent. They bore down upon us like horsemen of the apocalypse. I could hear you laughing at that. A little bit of melodrama. But it was true. What were the best areas to live in the town? What type of property were we searching for? How would we cope with all the removals?

I looked at my pale reflection. Despite the shimmering back and forth of people moving behind me it struck me how alone I was.

'I can do this,' I said. Then corrected myself guiltily. 'We can do this.'

I thought of the promises I'd made. To never stop thinking of you. To never stop talking about you. And us.

My old weary face peered at me. I wondered whether I had the energy, or the inclination, to climb the mountain on my own. The space beside me stretched away as if I was standing in the centre of a vast canyon. I was a tiny speck in a chasm.

I noticed then over my shoulder the friendly figure from the café. He bounded along the street with an enthusiastic zest for life. I turned to catch his eye, his presence giving me a fraction of hope that the task ahead was not insurmountable. But Wiktor had gone. He'd disappeared into the stream of passers-by.

I took a deep breath. 'I can do this,' I said. 'I will do this for us.'

And in a moment of determination, I reached out and pushed the door open.

3.

It was stuffy. There were four desks, each with a computer monitor and keyboard. Only one of the desks was occupied. It was neither modern or old fashioned. Oddly bland.

'My name's Rebekah,' she said slowly and loudly as if speaking to an elderly relative. She pointed to the name badge pinned to her blouse to reinforce her message.

'I'm Munro.'

'Mr Munro?'

'No,' I said. 'Just Munro'

Her hair was held back with a large maroon velvet clip. Her face was neatly made up giving her the appearance of a doll. She wore a corporate-looking red and blue chiffon scarf knotted, somewhat reluctantly, around her neck. I had the distinct feeling that I was being assessed. She looked at me with an owlish gaze more reminiscent of a librarian than an estate agent.

'How may I help?' she said with something of a sigh.

I sensed that perhaps the early career as an estate agent was not living up to Rebekah's expectations. Looking at the other desks, I wondered if her colleagues were out chasing listings and sales whilst she, as the junior, was left to the mundane tasks of answering the phones and dealing with inquisitive holiday-makers wanting to know what their money might buy them. But, more as likely, never would. This,

I reasoned, was the category she had placed me in.

'I hope you *will* be able to help me,' I said to her, hoping that she might warm to me on explaining my situation. 'I'm here to find a new home.'

She all but gave an exasperated eyeball roll. And in her defence, I could see that my statement was an obvious one.

'That's our business,' she said. *The glossy photos displayed in the window are a dead giveaway*, her look said.

I shuffled my feet on one of the grey nylon carpet tiles. This had not begun well. I could feel myself fighting off a mixture of anxiety and irritability. The office felt artificial. The sounds from outside were deadened by the double glazing and it felt as if I was hearing them under water.

'Perhaps I should explain.' I moved cautiously toward one of the chairs at her desk.

'Yes. If you could.' She sat rigid. Her large lashes blinked.

An invitation to take a seat was not offered so I hung awkwardly on to the back of one of the chairs.

'We accepted an offer on our house last week,' I said. I went on to detail where the house was located. To which the large lashes widened. A scarlet lipstick smile emerged to reveal a dazzling set of white teeth.

'Please do teak a seat, Mr Munro,' she said. The change in the atmosphere was palpable.

'It's just Munro.'

Her demeanour softened. It looked a relief for her to drop her barriers. At first, I wondered cynically whether the prospect of a sale was the cause of this sudden shift in personality. But as we proceeded, I became more convinced that she was grateful to find someone she could assist. A natural desire to help emerged, which appealed much more to me than the brittle business-façade I had first encountered.

'I've lived in Somerton-on-Sea all my life. So I'm a good person to show you the nicest areas. And those best to avoid.'

'You sound like an expert, Rebekah. Just the person required for the job.'

She bobbed enthusiastically in light of the praise. I could see why she had been employed.

'There is quite a lot of stock available but it's not exactly a buyer's market.'

'I see.' Except I didn't really.

'It will depend on the type of property you had in mind.'

An awkward pause punctuated the conversation. I had taken her comment as a statement rather than a question. 'What type of property?' I said.

'Yes,' she replied. 'Were you thinking of a house? And if so, would that be terraced, semi-detached or detached.'

'Ah, I see.'

'Or perhaps you have imagined a bungalow or a flat? All on one level and easy to maintain.'

'All things to consider.'

'Most out of towners have a picture in their mind's eye of a country cottage by the sea. You know the type of place. A whitewashed little house with roses growing over the front door.' She was painting a pretty picture. 'But the reality hardly ever lives up to the fantasy. So best to be realistic from the word go.'

I tried to think of what we had imagined. But again, those conversations felt so abstract now. It was all terribly wishy-washy. 'It's what I hoped you might be able to assist me with.'

'Yes, of course,' said Rebekah apparently relishing the prospect of starting with an absolute blank canvas. 'Perhaps we could start by you telling me the type of properties you've looked at online?'

I made myself comfortable on the chair. 'Online?'

'Yes,' she said nodding at her computer monitor.

'You make it sound like internet dating.'

She gave an unexpectedly throaty laugh. 'It doesn't matter if you haven't searched the website. It's just unusual these days, that's all. Most clients have seen something they like online.'

With a little encouragement and through the asking of relevant questions, I found myself outlining a potential list of criteria to Rebekah. Nothing too large. Nothing too small. Not on a busy road. But not too far from conveniences. Nothing overlooked. Nothing dark. Preferably a sunny aspect. A view would be nice. And somewhere to park the car.

Rebekah nibbled on the end of a pen as she typed the points into her computer. She was taking the task at hand seriously. Her brow furrowed as I spoke. 'Outside space?'

'Like a garden?'

'Could be. Or a balcony.'

'Somewhere to sit and have breakfast or coffee,' I said with unexpected, almost growing, certainty. 'But nothing too difficult to look after.'

'Container gardens are very on trend.'

'On trend. Yes.'

'And I do need to ask about finances,' she said sagely. I understood that discussing money could be something of a taboo, but Rebekah had scored points in my opinion for leaving this topic until my other priorities had been addressed. It reassured me that financial gain was not her only motive for assisting me. 'Some clients find it a bit awkward at this point. But it's the nature of the business so can't be avoided.'

I explained the situation. We had bought the house in 1981. The deposit had been possible through an inheritance and we had taken out the maximum mortgage available. The price of the house and the debt back then had been frightening. But we were young and had time on our side. We'd had no inclination that the area would become so desirable, but both agreed that it felt like a sound investment, which it had proved to be.

'It would be nice to release some of the capital,' I said. 'What's the point in having everything tied up in bricks and mortar when the cash could be used to make life a bit more comfortable?'

'Don't worry,' she said. 'Your budget will stretch further here.'

After quick consideration of the price range suggested by Rebekah, I gave a figure that we'd be happy with. 'There might be a bit more in the pot if we really have to.'

'That shouldn't be necessary.'

As she inputted the details into her computer, I remembered the excitement of buying a home together. Sliding that key into the front door for the very first time. Bounding from room to room with disbelief that it belonged to us – well, technically it was still the bank's – but in our hearts it was ours. It may as well have been yesterday; it was that clear.

How odd that it would soon be someone else's. The new owner was just a name on a piece of paper. I wondered whether we should have asked more about them? But it didn't seem relevant.

Rebekah gave a smile and nodded. 'I'm thinking of a few options.' She swivelled the computer monitor to face me and began to wave her pen in the direction of the screen. 'It's exciting!'

Exciting? Was that what this strange cocktail of emotions were? Excitement?

My face must have betrayed me as her cheeks flushed slightly, embarrassed that she may have unwittingly said the wrong thing.

'Yes. Exciting,' I replied, sounding unconvincing to myself.

She looked at me with that familiar pitying look. It was a look that said, 'How *sad*.' Or, 'How *lonely*.' For her, as a young woman, it probably seemed like an unfathomable amount of time.

I was grateful that she blustered lightly through

our awkward interlude. Something unspoken had passed between us, but she had not looked to expand or dwell upon it. Gently, but with a comforting self-assured manner, she looked at me and said, 'Let's take one step at a time. Firstly, this is what I'd suggest...'

A young family gathered around the telescope on the promenade. I watched as the mother played peek-a-boo with a young child in a buggy, their pleasure evident in unfettered shrieks of delight. The father was lifting his son to peer into the telescope. The boy's legs dangled and kicked with excitement.

I looked at the seafront panorama. The blue railings that edged the promenade tugged nostalgically at my heartstrings. The silhouette of the bandstand was defiantly unaltered by time. In fact, so little had changed of the view since my own childhood holidays.

The young family was moving on now. They held hands, lost entirely in their bubble.

I remembered my parents holding my hands. Swinging me into the air between them, trusting that they would never let me go.

'Nothing lasts forever,' Mum had said to me once. 'Neither the good nor the bad.'

Her words had stayed with me. For a long time they have lingered like an irrefutable truth. Perhaps she had been correct in that *things* don't last forever. But perhaps memories do?

I admonished myself for getting distracted by philosophical debates. It was not the time for being drawn off course. I had a mission. In my hand I clutched a bundle of particulars. Rebekah had handed them to me with the sensible advice of driving to look at each before deciding whether to view any of them.

'Get out and walk around a bit,' she'd said. 'It will help you get your bearings. You'll start to get a feel for the place.'

The town, she warned, might soon become grid-locked. So best to grab the bull by the horns. And, as she had foretold, on returning to the car I discovered that the carpark looked to be almost full to capacity. A warden dressed in a luminous vest marched ominously back and forth between the vehicles.

The morning was rapidly moving towards becoming the afternoon.

A pungent mixture of scents wafted over me. The salt of seawater. A fragrant whiff of seaweed. Something not quite possible to define, but definitely fishy. And possibly even the undertones of a chip shop. It could have all been bottled and sold as an aroma of the quintessential British seaside.

On reaching the car, I felt almost giddy with a sense of being part of it. The hotels on the seafront embodied the changing fortunes of holiday resorts. The sea itself, moving unflinchingly from low to high tide and back again, emphasised the constant unstoppable progress of time. It felt as if I had stepped out of my own life into that of a story.

Reversing the car from its space, the particulars on the passenger seat beside me, I was conflicted. Was I the author of this story? Or was it being written by somebody else? I followed the signs to the carpark exit and considered carefully whether to turn left or right.

4.

It was late afternoon by the time I squeezed into the small parking area of Haven Guesthouse. As I lugged my suitcase from the boot, I noticed dandelion seeds drifting in the breeze. On closer inspection I noticed nettles, brambles and the odd thistle.

I looked at the building. Its presence was as sturdy as I remembered. With its impressive lintels and large sash windows it still retained an air of an era when British seaside holidays still held some glamour. An overgrown creeper stretched to the slate roof on the nearest corner of the house. Random clumps of foliage peeked out from the gutters.

I had forgotten how much a part of the landscape it was, perched up high upon the eastern slopes of Somerton-on-Sea. It was as if it had been sculpted from the rocks beneath lunging out from the ground like a geological landmark.

Haven had been in the family for as long as I could remember. It originally belonged to my uncle Graham – my mother's brother – and his wife, Mary. I recall being told that it had been their dream. My memory of Graham was of a man who thrived on rules and routines. He was a stickler for detail and could appear abrupt, almost over-bearing, at times. Mary, on the other hand, I remembered as being almost ethereal. An ever-optimistic disposition endeared her to their visitors. Looking back, I realised what a formidable couple they had made. We all enjoyed their company and my mother, in particular, looked up to her elder brother and his wife with fond admiration.

They had twin daughters named Lana and Pearl who were some ten years my senior. I was shocked to think how old this made my cousins now. To me, they had just been the older girls who took me under their wings during our annual summer holidays, always willing to entertain my younger self with games of hide and seek around the grounds or scramble out with me to rock-pools on the coastline.

Standing in the shadow of it now, the link between now and then felt like a fragile strand of time. A series of disconnected recollections clamoured in my head, crashing down upon one another like waves on a beach. I heard the sound of shingle being dragged back into the sea.

I shivered.

A cloud had passed over the sun.

I suddenly felt a pressing need to understand the history of the place, as if it might reveal some hidden truth about myself. Time permitting, it would be the perfect opportunity.

I resolved to learn more about my family history before it was too late.

The large door with lead-light windows squeaked as I opened it. The brass door handle felt cold to touch. Dappled afternoon light filtered through tree branches and flickered on the flagstone paving. The sizeable porch was crammed with pelargoniums, vibrant in both colour and scent. On a shelf there stood a rack spilling over with pamphlets advertising tourist attractions and maps of the local area. I noticed too amongst the jumble, fliers from restaurants and pizza delivery companies.

Before even passing through the internal door to what I knew was the Reception, I heard what sounded like an altercation. I squinted through the mottled glass to see the vague shapes of those within.

With a sense of unease, I quietly opened the inner door to reveal the scene within. I took a pamphlet from the rack. My stealthy arrival saw me slip into the lobby unnoticed, allowing me to observe discreetly from a distance with the tourist literature in my hands as cover.

The Reception had the same floral carpet. It was worn and threadbare in places. And the dark wooden counter, which behind it hung numbered room keys on small hooks, was exactly as it had always been.

It was there that a man and woman were raising their voices to one of the landladies before them. 'Bloody hell, woman. Our booking clearly stated a *double* room,' he said. The interaction suggested a rapid escalation to a war of words. 'What kind of place are you running here?' At this point, his companion held her mobile phone out across the desk, thrusting its screen towards the bewildered face before them. 'Look! It's all there in black and white. It definitely says a *double room.*'

The couple shook their heads at one another.

'No wonder it was cheap,' he muttered under his breath.

So absorbed were they, that my presence had still gone unnoticed, and I began to feel uncomfortable. I didn't want to be caught out as voyeur. To avoid making an awkward situation any worse I gave a self-conscious sniff to announce myself.

The couple swung their heads towards me and froze in somewhat of a startled tableau.

I busied myself with the pamphlet which revealed itself to be advertising the local aquarium.

Either Lana or Pearl, I still had not confirmed to myself which yet, took a moment to register that the atmosphere had changed. She whispered something to herself as her gnarled fingers rifled at pages of scribbles before her. It was hard to hear what she was saying, but it sounded something like, 'I don't know how this could have happened.'

'Hello,' I said to the flushed faces of the couple.

He responded with a grunt.

'There seems to be a problem,' the woman beside him said.

At this, my cousin seemed to realise that the couple were addressing a third party. She lifted her head slowly and looked at them with a quizzical squint of incomprehension. Her gaze turned slowly in the direction they were looking until her spectacles glinted in my direction.

We locked eyes in some peculiar unspoken connection.

'Munro?' she said. 'Is it you?'

Before having an opportunity to reply, the door leading through to their private quarters opened and a replica of the flustered woman behind the desk emerged into the fray. The disgruntled couple looked taken aback as if their grievance had manifested an identical reserve on the elderly woman's behalf.

'I... I...' the man stuttered.

I was amused to see his confusion. It reminded me of the wicked games we had played as children. Confusing the adults as to which sister was which.

'Now, do you need a little help checking in?' she said, approaching the desk with the faintest of limps. It was this that identified her to me as Lana. She spoke as calmly as she ever did. 'We get so run off our feet during the festival week.'

'There appears to be some confusion,' the man said pompously as his companion bristled beside him. 'We booked a double room. We didn't ask for a *twin*.'

I noticed a reddening of his cheeks. His words had fallen flat in light of the identical faces before him.

Pearl had always been the powerhouse of the sisters with the same regimented discipline and self-confidence as her father. So it was a surprise to see her looking to Lana for guidance. She scratched her temple as if trying to clear a fuzz from her brain.

Lana scanned the page. 'Oh, I see what's happened,' she said lightly.

Pearl gawped. 'You do?'

'It's just a little clerical mistake. These things happen, don't they?'

The tension in the room had diffused in a flash

and within an instant the couple were engaged in amicable chit-chat about the festival. They looked like entirely different people as they laughed at how silly they had been to have been so het up. It wasn't like them at all, they said as the key to a double room was handed to them with information about the time breakfast was served in the morning and an insistence that they must ask if there was anything else that could be done to assist them during their visit.

Pearl noticed me as she had before. She nudged her sister. 'Munro's here.'

'And so he is,' said Lana.

It was not the room they had intended for me, Lana apologised. There had been a mix-up. There often were, she said, these days. It was the one I had stayed in as a boy, nestled up in the eaves. We would catch up on all the news, she said, once I'd had a chance to unpack my things and settle in. She had slipped away leaving me to take in my surroundings.

The room had shrunk since my childhood. Its sloping ceilings hovered precariously low above my head. A stain on the plasterwork looked to be the result of historic water damage. There were two single beds each with a mustard-coloured eiderdown. A shabby rug lay on the wooden floorboards. A decrepit trouser press looked decidedly out of place in the corner. I wondered who would be brave enough to plug it in.

A compact bathroom contained an avocado suite consisting of a toilet and tiny hand basin with a mirror above it. And a shower cubicle was concealed behind a flimsy plastic curtain.

It was of its day.

A fly droned a monotonous circle.

The window was open. It looked out across a shabby looking gable on which the askance tiles were covered with patches of moss. Through a canopy of foliage, the glimmer of the sea was just discernible. I heard a hum of activity in the distance, the prospect of things happening in the town below.

The windowsill had a thin layer of dust upon it.

I felt weary and sat upon one of the beds. It sagged ungraciously beneath me.

I thought of the particulars Rebekah had given me and tried to match them with my explorations of the day, but my tiredness rendered me useless. I fought my heavy eyelids as I thought of street signs and pavements and houses and flats.

What harm would it do just to lie down for a little while? I thought as I pushed off my shoes and lifted my legs on to the bed. It had been such an early start.

I lay my head on the pillow. And closed my eyes.

You looked so well. I was delighted. But shocked also, considering.

'Ambrose?'

'Of course,' you said. Your voice, which I was so frightened of forgetting, was exactly the same. You laughed and it made me feel both happy and sad. 'You look like you've seen a ghost.'

You wore jeans with red braces tight over a

white shirt. Your sleeves were rolled up as they always were. That was you, Ambrose. Always ready with your sleeves rolled up ready to fight the injustices of the world.

How handsome, I thought, you looked with your moustache.

The room smelt of stale cigarette smoke.

There were some discarded placards from a recent march. Posters emblazoned with slogans covered the walls. A radio was churning out ear worms.

It was the office. Up a narrow set of stairs above a launderette. Cobbled together with hand me down furniture: plastic chairs, a glass coffee table, filing cabinets. I noticed the leaflets with the phone number on it.

You sat at a desk. With a purpose. Just waiting.

You had faith. You said it would make a difference.

I went to speak to you. To ask what you had been doing. But the telephone began to ring. It looked like a museum-piece with its clunky dial.

As you were to do countless times over the years, you lifted the receiver and spoke to the caller. It might have been someone just wanting general information. Or someone in need of advice. Or someone on the edge. Or someone shouting abuse.

You were never phased. And I loved you for it.

I floated somewhere half-way between awake and asleep. It was a place in which you were still with me. And it was blissful.

And then I felt myself emerging from the

illusion.

I was coming round.

You were not here. The terrible empty horror of it hit me.

And it was like you had died all over again.

5.

The door to their private quarters stood slightly ajar but I was unsure as to whether I should enter or knock to make my presence known. It was early evening, and the place was in a quiet lull following the afternoon check-ins. Most guests had ventured out to explore the local restaurants.

'Hello?' I called out through the gap.

Footsteps approached. The door swung open.

'How long have you been waiting there?' said Pearl. 'We don't stand on ceremony here.'

I apologised and said I hadn't wanted to intrude, but she didn't appear to hear. 'I couldn't remember what the etiquette was.'

She gave a short huff. Again, I wasn't sure she had heard me, and I wondered whether age had diminished her hearing.

As I stepped over the threshold, it felt as if I had stepped back in time. The faded décor had not been updated in all these years. There was something about the way the light played against the walls that took me back to my childhood holidays. My mother had always said that the light was different at the coast.

'Have you been exploring?' she said but did not wait for me to reply. 'We don't go into town much.'

'Oh.'

'It's *changed*,' she said and wrinkled her nose. We moved through the hallway in the direction of a mouth-watering scent of home-cooked food.

'It used to be a sleepy little place, remember? Yes, we used to have the crowds at high season, but now its busy all year round.'

'Staycations?'

She wrung her hands and looked at me as if I was an imbecile.

'Too many people live here,' she said in rather an awkward accusing tone. 'That's the problem.'

'Munro!' said Lana as she appeared from the kitchen, a pink and white apron tied at her waist. She wore on her right foot a boot with a raised heel. A childhood condition had resulted in one of her legs being shorter than the other. It had never restricted her, but as a boy I had learnt that it was the quickest way to differentiate her from her twin.

I was relieved that her entrance had punctuated her sister's musings, but Pearl seemed determined to continue with her train of thought.

'Just telling him too many people live here.'

'The council can't win' said Lana lightly as if trying to gently swat away the conversation. 'They get criticised if the town doesn't attract enough tourists. They get criticised if they encourage second-home owners. And they get criticised if they build new homes for residents.'

'Too many people live here,' Pearl said again. I noticed that some of the buttons on her cardigan were done up in the wrong holes. I looked away quickly in fear of being caught staring. I felt I had seen something I shouldn't have.

A table was being laid.

'We don't have many guests for dinner,' said

Lana. 'It's a treat. I've baked a quiche. And there's salad. And new potatoes.'

We ate together in the easy way of those who have known each other a lifetime. But all the while we tip-toed around the potentially bigger conversations. We laughed about juvenile recollections of pranks we had played on our parents. And the time I had dragged a vast piece of driftwood back from the beach claiming that it looked like a dinosaur.

It was Lana who enquired as to my motive for wanting to move to Somerton-on-Sea. 'We were surprised,' she said. 'We always thought of you and Ambrose as town people.'

I was nervous about the topic of conversation.

'It was something we'd always talked about. Every time we'd had a day trip we'd tell each other how nice it would be to one day retire to the coast. It was a bit of a pipe dream, you might say.'

'You worked hard,' said Lana. 'You both did'.

I worried that I might get in too deep. I didn't want to make a fool of myself. 'We should have done it sooner. We didn't get the timing right.'

'But you are doing it now.'

Pearl stood abruptly. Her chair scraped. 'These dirty plates won't clear themselves away.'

'Was there ever someone special for you?' I asked.

Lana looked over her shoulder. Pearl had moved through to the lounge and was shouting answers at a quiz show on the television. Confident that she was out of earshot, Lana said,

'There was a boy once. We were very young. And, as you expressed so well, the timing was all wrong.'

She had her hands deep in the washing up suds. She gazed wistfully out of the window. I did not want to disturb her reverie by probing for more details despite my curiosity. She wiped a plate before rinsing it under the tap and handing it to me.

I felt its warmth through the old tea towel.

'I heard some people talking on the radio the other day. I like to listen as I'm doing the daily chores. They were discussing holidays. And one of them said that the best thing about having a holiday is the coming back home again.' She gripped the edge of the sink in her marigolds. 'They said that after seeing how other people live you return to your life with a new set of eyes. To see things from a fresh perspective.'

'Yes, I suppose that might be true,' I said not entirely sure where her train of thought was heading.

'They said that it was in the going home that you were able to evaluate the life choices you had made and truly see what your life had become.'

I thought about the house I'd left this morning. Was this what she was referring to? Was she suggesting that upon my return I might have cold feet about the path I was embarking on?

'Do you think I might be making a mistake?' I asked.

'A mistake?'

I had misunderstood. I could see in her eyes that she had not been referring to me. On comprehending, I said, 'Wouldn't it have just felt like a busman's holiday?'

She laughed wanly. 'But don't you see? It wasn't the lack of holidays I envied. It was the possibility of returning.'

I must have been in my early teens when it happened. Which would have made the twins in their early twenties.

I only knew scant details. Their parents had always enjoyed swimming in the sea. It was something they did together. I could picture them in my mind's eye: Mary's bright swimming hat bobbing along the surface as she did breaststroke, and Graham's tanned arms pulling him along in a crawl.

They thought they knew the sea. They had swum in it so many times. They were experienced. But on that occasion one of them had 'got into trouble'. Those were my mother's words. With hindsight, I suppose it meant that they had got caught in a rip or an undercurrent. Or, thinking of you, perhaps one of them had become unwell.

I imagined it being scrawly and the seafront deserted. Their distant cries for help lost in the murk. A heap of clothes and towels abandoned on the damp pebbles.

As a family we didn't talk about it, so it might not have been like this at all. I only really remember being shocked. A disbelief that two people I knew so well had gone in their prime. It was my first experience of loss. And it had been brutal.

Lana must have sensed what I was thinking

about. 'The guesthouse was *their* dream.'

'And did you feel obliged to honour that for them?'

'Perhaps,' she said. 'It was all so sudden and unexpected. Life came off the tracks like a train derailment. I suppose us taking on the business was a way of keeping them alive.'

Her words resonated with me. Wasn't this the very reason that had brought me here?

'It must have been so difficult for you both.'

'Yes. But we had each other. We shared the burden.'

Burden? Was that, I wondered, how Lana saw a lifetime at Haven Guesthouse? A life spent fulfilling someone else's dream?

Pearl barked at the television again, her voice louder than before. Her random words made the place feel unsettled. There was something of the asylum about it.

I was struck by the complexity of their relationships. With each other. With their parents. With the guesthouse.

The ghosts lingered.

'Oh, we've become gloomy,' said Lana. The eternal optimism I knew her for was attempting to return, but it shone a little less bright than it once had. 'Come and tell us more about your plans. Let's hear what you have in mind.'

The promenade was buzzing with dog-walkers, joggers and those – like me – just taking an evening stroll.

I had not taken offence at Lana and Pearl declining my invitation to join me. The guesthouse was a vast undertaking. One that, at their advancing years, was taking a toll. I thought of two old hamsters on a wheel and wondered how long they could keep it up for.

I was glad to have time to myself. I breathed in the sea air deeply and hoped that it would garner me with strength and perseverance. The quest to find a suitable home had only just begun.

'Munro?'

I jolted from my ruminations. To hear my own name being called surprised me.

At first, I could not see who had called my name. All the faces were unfamiliar. And I wondered whether I had misheard.

'Munro! It's you!'

'Wiktor?' I said. It was the jovial Polish man I'd encountered at the café.

'Yes! You remember my name!' He sat on one of the benches that looked out to the waves.

I approached and saw that he sat beside an elderly man who had a tartan blanket draped over his knees. There was a walking frame on the ground beside him.

'You are staying near here?' Wiktor asked.

I explained that I was staying with my cousins. 'They have a guesthouse up on the hill called Haven.' I nodded in its direction.

At this, the frail old man turned his watery eyes upon me and scrutinised me. 'Your cousins?' he croaked.

'Yes,' I replied.

I thought I saw his white eyebrows raise slightly.

'This is Sandy,' said Wiktor.

'My name is Sandy,' the man echoed.

'I help him wash and get dressed in mornings. Help him put on pyjamas at bedtime. And on some evenings, we walk. Not far. It takes time. But I am patient.' He gave a proud smile. 'I like to help. Getting old is not for wimps.'

Sandy listened as Wiktor enquired after my house hunting. I explained that progress was slow but that I was hopeful in finding just what I wanted. It had only been a day, but Somerton-on-Sea was already starting to feel a little bit like home.

'I've lived here all my life,' said Sandy.

'And you've been happy?' I asked.

'Every life has its challenges. But I wouldn't have wanted to have faced them anywhere but here. I'm like a stick of seaside rock. If you snapped me in half, you'd find 'Somerton-on-Sea' written all the way through me.'

Wiktor laughed. 'Sandy has a good sense of humour.'

'It has a reputation as being somewhat of a God's Waiting Room,' said Sandy. 'But that's not very fair.'

I looked at his stooped posture. He looked fragile, almost in danger of turning to dust. The contrast between him and Wiktor beside him was stark.

A cyclist swerved around me with a tinkle on their bell.

'Haven Guesthouse you say?'

'Yes,' I replied.

'I see.' He began to fold the blanket up slowly. His fingers white and tiny. 'I see.'

He struggled to his feet with assistance and grabbed the metal frame beside him. This movement alone left him panting. Then with unexpected vigour he set off along the prom.

'Inner strength, eh?' said Wiktor, looking on at his companion with admiration. 'Will be seeing you again, Munro.' It was said as a statement of fact with absolutely no uncertainty. 'Will be seeing you again!'

6.

That night, my sleep was unsettled. My body was too big for the narrow single bed which was strangely lumpy in places and my outstretched limbs would not settle and dangled over the edge. I wished I had brought my own pillows from home with those provided being old and thin. I would have a kink in my neck in the morning.

The room was airless despite my attempts to jam the window open as far as it would go.

I drifted in and out of dreams that made no sense. They had no logic like the type of rambling tales told by children which are just a series of events rather than there being any sequential cause and effect. A babbling splurge of disconnected things.

I hovered somewhere between awake and asleep. Each time my eyes opened I was confronted by the red digits of an ancient clock radio. The minutes crept forward.

I thought I heard the sound of footsteps on floorboards and doors being closed. But I could not be sure. The building creaked and thudded. Sometimes the pipes rattled or whooshed as a distant toilet was flushed. At one point, I could almost make out a muffled conversation being held but the voices only reached me as a series of mumbles.

During one of the dreams, I was back at the guesthouse as a boy. My parents were still alive. And I was running on the beach; my arms and legs powering me along. My bare feet splashed on the wash, and I could feel the sand between my toes. But then I saw you on the promenade waving joyfully at me, which didn't make sense as you were an adult. And then I saw my parents wading fully-clothed into the sea. I had not known whether to look at them or you. And then the woman from the high street who wore a camel coat and walked her little dog was balancing on one of the barnacle-encrusted groynes.

I woke with a groan. My aching bones were entangled in the sheet. I thrashed my legs to try and release myself.

I cursed at having become old and grumpy.

Had the spirit of that young boy in the dream been lost? I wondered. It was a depressing thought and I tried to suppress it.

I rolled on to my back with a huff. I tried to concentrate on my breathing in order to clear my head. But however hard I tried, I could not prevent the anxieties scrolling through my brain. The house was sold. And I was as yet no closer to finding a new home.

What had possessed me to embark upon this change?

Was it a promise I had made to you?

Looking back, like the unsettling dreams, doesn't always make sense. The order in which things happened, or whether in fact they ever happened at all, I can't be sure of.

The image of Pearl and the mismatched buttons on her cardigan sprung into my mind's eye.

Everything, it seemed, had become rather a jumble.

On the morning of day one hundred and eighty-six, having shaved and negotiated the temperamental shower, I emerged – somewhat groggily – from my room to a scene of towels and sheets being deposited into a vast basket. It was a flurry of white laundry.

I could not disguise my surprise when the linen descended to reveal a face I recognised.

'Wiktor?'

'Munro!' he said. 'I said I would see you again soon. And sooner than you think, eh?' he winked.

'You work here too?'

'I do.' He pushed out his chest. 'Every morning after I visit Sandy, I come here for a couple of hours. Then on to the café.'

I was impressed by his work ethic.

He shook a sheet before stuffing it into the basket. 'It is good to work. I came from Poland to build a better life for myself.'

'Have you lived here long?'

'A few years now.'

'And do you miss Poland?'

'There is no place like home,' he said. 'But Somerton-on-Sea is a good place and friendly people. There is opportunity here if you choose to see it.'

I liked his turn of phrase.

He paused for a moment from his task at hand. 'It's funny, but sometimes when I work I think about my old country and it seems that I am still there. How would you say? Like I live a *parallel* life.'

I thought of the empty house and wondered whether a version of me was still there. I pictured myself wandering alone from room to room. It was a ridiculous idea.

'Lana and Pearl must appreciate you.'

'They need the extra pair of hands,' he said sagely. 'They struggle to cope.'

I suddenly feared that our conversation might be over-heard. I wouldn't want to be seen as passing judgement on my cousins' situation.

Seeming to understand my desire for discretion, Wiktor lowered his voice and said, almost conspiratorially, 'They are kind people. They give me clear instructions on how to do the job well. But sometimes I do things to make jobs quicker and do not tell them.' He raised a finger to his lips to indicate this was our secret.

'I expect they are used to doing things a certain way. They have done this for a very long time.'

'Exactly, yes. And I respect that.' He looked as if he was trying to gather his thoughts. 'Apologies. It's not always easy with language.'

'You speak English very well,' I said.

'Let me see, how you say,' he replied, 'life is always moving forward. Like it or not. And if we are not open to change, we *die*.' He shoved a handful of towels into the basket and laughed. 'Too serious a conversation for before breakfast!'

'Not at all,' I said, my stomach turning its attention to being fed. 'I love to listen.'

'You are a good listener. Just don't forget to speak.'

As I made my way down the stairs, I wondered

what he meant.

I entered the breakfast room to the sound of murmured voices. It looked smaller than I recalled with the guests crammed in at the available tables. And like everything else I'd encountered, it seemed not to have been altered by the passage of time. The walls were covered in magnolia wood-chip wallpaper and furnished with framed watercolour paintings; romanticised scenes of Somerton-on-Sea that had been bleached by sunlight. A cobweb swung lazily from the light fitting on the ceiling. The same heavy velvet drapes had been pulled back to reveal the French windows propped open to the flagstone patio beyond.

I nudged my way apologetically across the room to an available table in the corner. Navigating by protruding elbows and errant handbags, I mumbled vague good mornings to those I passed. It all felt cramped.

As I took my seat, I sensed the eyes of those around me taking me in. I scanned the room quickly intrigued as to who had chosen to stay here, but their close proximity made it feel as if I was intruding. I did, in this brief surveillance, catch sight of the couple who had been disgruntled whilst checking-in yesterday. They sat stony-faced in each other's company.

I looked away.

The sky was cloudless. I took this as a good omen for my day of property-hunting ahead. I could see beyond the shrubbery and treetops a glimpse of the town below. The white tips of gull wings in flight flashed against the blue.

Having undertaken my initial reconnaissance of the locale, my plan for the day was to arrange viewings of the shortlist I'd made of potential properties. I had no particular front-runner. Instead, I vowed to keep an open mind. To be open to the possibility of being surprised.

I looked at my watch. I would have to keep focused or the day would slip away.

The sound of rumbling dissatisfaction caught my attention.

I noticed that the stony-faced couple now had Lana standing beside their table, two plates aloft. The pair shook their heads and rolled their eyeballs.

Lana turned and proffered the cooked breakfasts with no avail to the other guests. She noticed me and acknowledged me with a quick embarrassed smile then retreated back to the swinging door of the kitchen.

What had been a gentle murmur was rapidly increasing to a simmering grumble of discontented voices. The tension was only brought to an abrupt silence by the crash of something being dropped and smashing in the kitchen.

The breakfast room froze. Its occupants looked at one another wide-eyed.

Frustration had given way to furtive whispered curiosity. Almost, I feared, a morbid fascination.

I didn't want to sit and watch the show.

It was a snap decision. I got to my feet and zig-zagged through the astonished faces.

I had not expected the chaos that greeted me in

the kitchen. Strewn around were loaves of bread, egg cartons and a plethora of kitchen utensils.

The cousins were locked in some sort of strange paralysis. They stared at the tiled floor where the remains of a broken plate and the food which had been upon it lay in a messy splatter.

'*How* could the order be *wrong*?' said Pearl. Her tone struck me as uncomfortably aggressive towards her sister. She looked unkempt. Her hair looked as if it had been brushed at a strange angle.

'Let's not get ourselves upset,' Lana soothed. 'These things happen,'

I gave an awkward shuffle regretting having left my table.

Pearl snapped her face in my direction. 'What do *you* want? Come to tell us *your* order is wrong too I suppose.'

'It's Munro,' Lana said.

Pearl steadied herself. 'I know who it is.'

I wasn't sure. She had recovered quickly. But I wasn't convinced she had recognised me.

'Can I...'

'We don't need you upsetting the apple cart,' Pearl said to me. 'How many years have we done this for now? We don't need somebody telling us how to do things.'

'Nobody's telling anybody how to do things,' said Lana. 'Munro just wants to help. Isn't that right?'

I nodded.

Pearl looked unconvinced.

Lana held a dustpan and brush. 'Let's just clear things up and then take one thing at a time.'

As Pearl stomped back and forth aimlessly with a cloth, I attempted to create some order from the chaos by clearing the pans on the stove and tidying the ingredients and plates. Lana cleaned up the spillage on the floor and when Pearl wasn't looking mouthed me a silent thank you.

Her eyes were sunk into dark rings. I saw how stooped she had become and how thin she looked. She scraped the contents of the dustpan wearily into the bin.

I was suddenly aware of Pearl's presence at my shoulder. Her laboured breath was against my ear. 'You gave up the fight,' she whispered. 'You let it defeat you.'

I turned. She looked hollow to me.

Her eyes met mine, but I had an odd sensation that there was nothing behind them.

'Good job he's not here to see it,' she said. 'He wouldn't wanted to have seen you let the side down.'

I was aghast.

This was not the Pearl I had known. This was not the girl who had encouraged me to join her in climbing the rocks at the foot of the cliffs. And certainly not the bounding force of energy she had been.

This Pearl was brittle.

I tried to look casual as I attempted to place the orders written on scraps of paper into some kind of order, but I noticed that my hands were trembling. The slips fluttered from my fingertips, and I could sense Pearl's myopic disgust glaring at me.

As Lana re-joined us to make a trio, I wondered

whether I should confront Pearl on what she had said. But, unlike the past, I could not be sure of her reaction. This Pearl was volatile and uneasy. Not a bit like the dependable stoic Pearl I had once known.

Now was not the right time to address the elephant in the room. Not with a room full of impatient hungry guests.

I rolled up my sleeves to muck in. And hoped that Lana hadn't seen me looking anxiously at the time on my watch.

7.

As I scurried purposefully away from the guesthouse, I felt guilty at how relieved I was to be escaping its confines. I looked at it in the rear-view mirror and tried to spirit up the childhood version I had so frequently fantasised about. But the ominous cloud that hung over its owners cast an unshakeable shadow over the whole place. It was as if the sun had been taken from the sky.

The weather wasn't helping to lift my melancholy mood either. It had grown humid. I wound down a window and felt the damp sticky air upon my skin. My clothes clung to me.

The events of the morning lingered just beneath the surface. I could sense them threatening to pop up and re-play on repeat in my thoughts. I could smell the cooked breakfasts still. The crackle of frying was in my ears. The cooking fat lingered on me, stale and greasy.

I wondered when things had become so difficult for them. The occurrences I had witnessed since my arrival had not appeared surprising to them. I suspected that the change they were experiencing, unlike my own, had been a gradual decline. A slow changing of things like waves eroding a cliff. The sort of change that is imperceptible. Creeping upon them like an unwanted guest.

I suppose they'd held some solace in clinging to their familiar surrounds. Easier, perhaps, to fight the battle on their own territory. To view an attempt at maintaining a status quo as a strategy.

This, I surmised, was what Pearl's outburst at me had meant. And as such, I felt justified in dismissing her comments as more of a reflection of their own situation than mine.

She had said more about herself than about me. That's what I decided.

I wiped moisture from my forehead with the back of my hand. There was a dull ache in my head.

I needed to think clearly today.

I forced myself back into an established pattern, dealing with things in my own particular way. I had been vaguely aware of this in the past. But since it happened, my approach to things – my coping mechanisms, you might say – were much more apparent to me. Keep busy. Be sure to have a plan for the day ahead. Try and account for every hour.

By keeping my attention occupied, I figured, there was less chance of me being undone by what had come before.

It was Rebekah, whom I had insisted with the agency be the representative to show me around my shortlist of properties, who greeted me on the narrow pavement. Away from the office and in the natural light she looked younger than I recalled. And no doubt in reverse, my age was now more than apparent to her.

Her face was as immaculately made up as before and she wore the same business attire.

She shook my hand.

'Before we take a look at this one,' she said, 'I need to update you on the maisonette on Kings

Street.' The photos on the particulars had shown a light and airy three bedroomed property with high ceilings and original sash windows. I had already ear-marked it as a potential front-runner. This was due to be our final viewing of the afternoon. 'The owners have accepted an offer on it. So, unfortunately, we won't be looking at it.'

It was disappointing but I had vowed to be pragmatic.

'Que se ra,' I said, thinking fondly of the song and how you loved to bellow it.

Rebekah's face showed no sign of comprehension. 'Sometimes these things happen for a reason,' she said matter-of-factly.

'Maybe they do.'

I had no intention of telling her, but I was trying to pick up on any potential signs from you that might indicate which decision I should take. I had asked you in the car not to be shy about providing any messages as to what the right thing to do might be.

Rebekah rummaged in her bag and extracted a set of keys.

It was a mid-terrace house. A shabby little space of paving slabs stood at its frontage behind a crumbling white rendered wall. To call it a garden would be optimistic.

'It's been a rental for several years,' said Rebekah. 'I think you might say it's a bit tired but got potential. It's vacant now and all the furniture has been removed.'

The front door opened immediately on to a bland sitting room. I was thrown by its emptiness. I scanned the blank walls. Hooks remained where picture frames had once hung. The window had a venetian blind. There was a dusty grey gas heater in the fireplace. I noticed on the brown carpet the imprints of where furniture had previously stood. Probably a sofa, a coffee table, a TV stand.

'It needs a bit of imagination,' said Rebekah. 'A bit of vision.'

I had the silly feeling that my initial reaction had disappointed her. I tried to think of something positive to say to make her feel better but found myself incapable of raising any enthusiasm. It was impossible to feign any excitement. I heard myself muttering and falling over my own words.

'Why don't you look around upstairs on your own? I'll meet you when you're done out the back.'

I was glad of the opportunity to be alone.

The staircase led up to a landing and three soulless bedrooms. The floorboards creaked as I moved about. I noticed that even the lamp fittings had been removed leaving just the lightbulbs.

'Well?' I said. 'Aren't you going to say anything?'

But you didn't answer.

I looked around for a sign that you might even be listening. But the empty rooms just swept around me.

For a terrible moment I wondered whether you had ever existed at all. Perhaps I had just made you up. Perhaps you had been nothing more than a glorious invention.

The bathroom smelt stale. A discoloured bathmat hung limply over a radiator. Of all the things to have left, I thought. And on the basin, there was the cracked remains of an old bar of soap. I stared at it in fascination. Here I was, meant to be looking at one of life's most expensive purchases, instead staring at the hair of a stranger stuck to a bar of soap.

Rebekah insisted that I should not despair. It was after all only the first viewing. It would, she said, be unlikely to find what I wanted at a first attempt.

As we moved on to the next viewing, the first of three more, I began to panic that the search would defeat us. I made a futile attempt at trying to put the list of priorities into an order of importance. Without your input I felt unsure as to what mattered most to us. Which in turn made me feel despondent about how well I had known us at all.

I could almost hear you saying that there would have to be compromises.

All well and good telling me that now. But you hadn't said that when we'd talked about it in the past. There had only been unwavering perfection and golden sunsets. Somerton-on-Sea had been an idyll.

There came a distant rumble of thunder. It echoed through the streets and provoked the gulls into a chorus of manic wails. I imagined that the sound was actually that of vast cogs shifting beneath us. They were grinding against one another as components in a machine. A machine that dictated time and destiny, on which we were merely its automaton characters.

Not for the first time, I felt abandoned.

In all the swirling emotions and feelings I'd encountered, anger and frustration were the ones that I felt least comfortable admitting to. How could you have left me? How dare you? Why hadn't you left me with instructions about how to carry on? Sometimes it struck me that it was easier for you. And that I envied you for being the first to go. You no longer had to think about the mundane practicalities.

I felt a few large spots of rain. They splashed wetly onto the warm plants and concrete causing an earthy aroma to lift into the air.

As on previous occasions, my brief anger at you turned quickly to feeling guilty. You wouldn't see the rain again. You wouldn't hear it smattering down.

There was a future of things that you would never see.

It was, I reminded myself, the very reason why I was here in Somerton-on-Sea. It was why I was on this merry dance with an estate agent. It was a promise I had made to honour our plan. A determination to live the future we had dreamt about together.

As the day progressed, Rebekah and I dodged our way through the rain showers. She held her blazer above her head to protect her hair and make-up. I battled with a belligerent umbrella.

I had not expected each home to be so different. Each had its own character as if it was a living being in its own right. It was a rare experience of stepping into other people's lives to see how they live. Some were neat and minimalist. Others hoarded. Some had modern furniture whilst others had antique pieces.

What had they thought about our own home? Had they, like me, already in their imaginations been making alterations and changes?

As we weaved our way through gathering footfall for the festival, I congratulated myself on keeping up with Rebekah. My 'to do list strategy' was serving me well. I was relieved to have asked for back-to-back viewings. In travelling straight from one place to the next, it meant that there was no time to over-think things.

And at this speed, I was confident I could outrun the dread of loneliness.

If it was lingering in the crowds, I had not seen it.

From the bench I had chosen, I scanned the panorama.

The soft edge of falling waves were far away. The tide was as far out as it could be creating a grand sweep of beach on which people looked like stick figures on a painting. Puffs of cloud looked to be remnants of the stormy day.

I cradled the warm package of fish and chips on my lap and tackled it with a small wooden fork. The threat of a scavenging bird hovered ominously around me.

On returning to the guesthouse, I had felt weary. Lana had intercepted me in Reception. I sensed that she had been waiting for my return.

She claimed that she was waiting for more guests to check-on, but I think she had been lingering. She thanked me again for stepping into the breach that morning. I told her to think nothing of it and that it seemed like a long time ago.

'How did you get on?' she'd asked tentatively. 'I was thinking about you.'

It had been a bit of a whirlwind, I explained. I told her about the maisonette that had already received an offer and the initial despair I had felt at the first vacant property. But the estate agent had been patient with me. She had not hurried me.

I heard myself saying the word '*me*'. I felt self-conscious about it. It sounded harsh. Me. Me. Me.

She seemed genuinely interested in hearing about the other properties of which one I paid particular attention in describing.

'Is it what Ambrose would have wanted?' she asked.

'I think it's what we would have chosen together. It's very *us*.'

It was contrary, but I wanted to be alone. Just some time to gather my thoughts. I said to Lana that I would make my own arrangements for supper. She understood. She was pleased, she said, that the day had been a success.

I stabbed the fork into a fat chip.

The vendors would consider the offer overnight.

Tomorrow morning I – sorry, we – would have an answer.

8.

On day one hundred and eighty-seven, I encountered the full thrust of the festival.

There was a freshness to the new day. The moisture from yesterday's downpours hadn't entirely evaporated but it no longer sat humidly in the air. Instead, it glistened on the promenade railings and shone on the tarmac. It felt crisp. I breathed it in and felt invigorated.

My mobile phone was in my jacket pocket. The answer had not come yet. But I didn't feel unduly concerned. Rebekah had said that the owners weren't always easy to contact. I guessed they had busy working lives or perhaps lived abroad. Rebekah hadn't expanded. It was all just part of the process. Besides, I was half-expecting my initial offer to be rejected. It had merely been a starting point. A suitable place to begin a negotiation.

I weaved a path through the chattering masses who appeared to be gathering along the pavements for some anticipated spectacle. Bunting had been strung up between the lamp posts and flapped noisily in the breeze. Some of the roads had been cordoned off with signs diverting traffic to alternative routes. The absence of motor engines somehow exaggerated the voices around me.

Animated children were being clung to by their hands of their nearest and dearest. In places, I noticed that they were even being balanced on shoulders to get a better perspective on the unfurling scene.

Whether it was the decisive step forward in having made an offer or just the consequence of absorbing myself in the place, I suddenly felt optimistic about Somerton-on-Sea. I seemed on the verge of becoming part of it. Not just a fleeting tourist or by-stander.

In the distance came the rhythmic sound of drums being struck, a cacophony of music and the piercing trill of whistles being blown.

I felt a ripple of excitement run through the crowd. There was clapping and pointing of fingers.

There seemed something serendipitous about this unexpected encounter. It was an opportune moment to witness another side to the town.

I took up a vantage point on a grimy set of steps. From the raised position I could see an approaching flotilla of decorated floats. Flat-backed lorries were decorated in various scenes. The participants on them and those accompanying them on the road were dressed in outrageous and fanciful costumes.

I couldn't fathom a coherent theme. There were mermaids and chimney sweeps. A group of boys twirling batons marched to disco. A fire engine draped in tinsel hooted its horn and gave blasts on its siren.

'It's to mark the summer solstice!' somebody shouted.

I looked at the psychedelic stream of residents. A choir passed by attempting to sing in competition with the roar around it. There were community groups of various sizes. Some were small in number and wore sashes. Others were larger and marched with banners.

A gaggle of drag queens tottered by in sequined knee-high boots. Their bouffant wigs made them look incredibly tall. They engaged joyfully with their observers. And in their wake rippled a veritable sea of rainbow flags.

It was you.

I wobbled for a second.

Of course it wasn't you.

But he had looked like you, majestically waving a spectacularly big flag from side to side as if at the peak of the barricades. This morning he was not folding laundry, or taking orders at the café, or helping an old man get dressed.

He did not see me.

I watched him go by with a possessive type of pride.

Had I needed any other sign this morning that the cogs beneath the ground were turning in my favour as the carnival rescinded, I saw through my watery eyes the crowd ahead dissipate to reveal the glass frontage of a shop. Beneath its signage spun red and white. Through its reflection, there were chairs facing mirrors and a black and white chequered floor.

'Oh,' I whimpered.

The dispersing throng was getting quieter, but they were too preoccupied to notice a white-haired fool stifling his sobs. They were focused on their next destination.

I made myself look. How long I had avoided confronting any of it. Too afraid that it would drag me into the terrifying bottomless pit. To be pulled beneath its whirling depths.

All too aware was I that since it had happened, my emotions had been heightened. As if someone had turned up the dial on them. And when left unchecked, they had been in constant danger of gushing out like a torrent of water from a burst pipe.

The people around me had gone. It was time to move on.

Surely it had to be some kind of a message?

'God only knows what our father would have made of it all. I mean, look at the state of it.'

I had returned to find Lana kneeling on a cushion at the over-grown garden bed beside the entrance to Haven. She wore stained gloves that had seen better days and a petite sun hat perched on her head. 'He always managed to keep things looking perfect.'

'I remember,' I said.

'Particular about everything, wasn't he? It all had to be just so.' She plunged a wooden-handled trowel into the soil. 'It's hard to tell where the weeds stop and the plants begin.' She dislodged a specimen and looked curiously at it for a second before flinging it on to a brimming trug. 'He'll be turning in his grave.'

I remembered then my previous determination to find out more about our family history. It had slipped from my mind.

Had Graham and Mary been recovered from the sea? Had they been buried? Or had their grave been a metaphorical watery one?

Lana pushed herself slowly and unsteadily up

on to her uneven legs. I shadowed her not knowing whether to offer assistance or not. I opted just to hover close by and chose not to ask for the grim details about her parents. It wasn't the right time. Perhaps, I wondered, it never would be.

She brushed dirt from her skirt and placed her hands on her hips. We stood together and looked at what she had achieved. It had made a difference. The shrubs were neatly shaped and space between them gave them a tidy prominence.

'Something to be said for first appearances,' she said.

I thought of the properties I'd viewed. How true it was.

We paused. The face of the building loomed down on us. I looked up from the border and scanned the peeling paintwork. Tendrils from the creeper seemed to reach out to us. I dreaded to think of what unseen damage it might be doing to the building.

'I do have fond memories of our holidays here,' I said.

'Frightening to think how long ago that was.'

'Does it feel like such a long time?'

She considered the question. 'Yes and no.'

I understood.

Lana gathered up her gardening tools. I picked up the trug.

We continued to reminisce as we traced the wild uneven path that led around the building.

'They were special times for us too,' she said.

We stepped gingerly upon the ragged ground. I

let her talk. In listening, I hoped that some nuggets of family history might be revealed.

'I suppose part of it was it being school holidays. That feeling of freedom. The prospect of a summer stretching endlessly ahead. But there was more to it than that. When you and your parents came to visit it felt *different*.'

'Different?' I asked. 'In what way?'

'Well, it's difficult to explain. Growing up here, the boundaries between life and work were a bit blurry. And whilst there was never a shortage of things happening, the days did tend to roll into one. But your annual stays felt like punctuation marks. Our parents, father in particular, seemed more relaxed when you stayed. It was as if he let us off the leash. Maybe he let himself off the leash too.'

I thought of Graham's strict routines. I could picture him even now tirelessly working through his gruelling regime. If that had been him being relaxed, I couldn't imagine how it must have been around him when he was at full throttle.

'There are so many reminders of them here,' I said.

'That's true. Sometimes I feel like they're still about, roaming the old place. Horrified, no doubt, at what it looks like now.'

We had made our way to the greenhouse whose wooden frame was rotten in places and remaining panes of glass were stained with a green slime. Nothing but weeds grew within. Used now only for storage.

'We should have done what you're doing,' she said.

'Moved?'

'Yes. Down sized. Isn't that the expression?' She began to mindlessly tidy a stack of abandoned flowerpots. 'Looking back, we should have done it years ago. Hindsight's a wonderful thing, eh?'

'It's never too late.'

I watched as her sorting of the pots slowed. I wasn't going to press her on the subject, but I sensed that she wanted to say more so I waited patiently. She began to flitter around the interior of the greenhouse. It brought to mind a trapped faded butterfly, looking unsuccessfully for an escape.

'We hardly noticed it at first,' she said. 'It was just little things like forgetting to buy certain groceries, or not remembering where she had left her specs. It was just getting old, we had said. We had even laughed about it.'

I thought of the mismatched buttons I had seen on Pearl's cardigan.

Lana looked directly at me. 'Have you noticed a difference in her?'

'I wasn't sure.' I hoped my answer was oblique enough. I was feeling guilty for not having visited them more often. They were the only family I really had.

'That's good, I suppose. We try to hide it well. Keeping to the same routines each day helps. Doing the things that we have always done. She knows her way around the place well enough. I leave her little notes to remind her of things.'

'I hadn't realised it was so bad.' I wondered what it would feel like to see a version of yourself disappearing.

'It is what it is,' she said stoically. 'I try to hold on to the glimpses of the Pearl I know. But every day those glimpses become rarer. It's as if she's slipping away.'

I felt her and my loss keenly; both real and ambiguous.

'It's not just taking her memory,' Lana said. 'It's taking her character.'

I was scrambling in my head to try and find the words. What was the right thing to say?

I tried to remember the well-meaning words that had been said to me but could only recall those that had upset me such as: 'At least you had all those years together. How lucky you were...'

Carefully, I said, 'You don't have to cope on your own.'

That fragile thread glistened between us. A lifetime of connection.

The dank air was suddenly filled with an unexpected piercing melody. We looked – confused - at one another and around us to see where the tune was coming from.

'My phone!' I said as I fumbled in my pocket to answer it.

Following our conversation, I hadn't wanted to add to her worries. She had enough concerns of her own.

'Is everything okay?' she'd asked warily.

I tried to make light of it. During the telephone conversation I withdrew from the greenhouse. I stumbled deeper into the garden keeping my voice low. I wasn't sure how much she had heard. Probably enough.

Whilst I didn't want to leave Lana alone, I knew that I needed a moment to myself.

I sensed her eyes pursue me as I bid a swift retreat to my room where, having wheezed up the staircase, I found myself pressed with my back against the door gasping for breath.

She was very sorry, Rebekah had said. It was a bolt out of the blue. The vendors situation had changed. They were no longer in a position to be able to sell. There was nothing we could do about it, she said. She was very, very sorry. We would have to go back to the drawing board.

At least I had some viewings under my belt now, she said.

But as far as I was concerned, it was back to square one.

I looked back and forth between the two single beds.

The tentative hopeful prospects I had felt earlier in the day were gone.

None of the other properties would do.

'Well, are you going to say anything?' I said looking up at and beyond the cracked ceiling. 'Isn't it about time you spoke?'

The room was still.

I waited.

And waited.

And then, to my surprise, a knock came at the door.

9.

Ambrose was a man who got things done. Life was not a dress rehearsal. It was to be grabbed fiercely with both hands like a rugby ball and hurtled down the pitch. Failure was not a word in his vocabulary. Any obstacle, he insisted, could be overcome through enthusiasm and persistence.

He was a natural leader. His self-confidence and stature endeared others to him and his causes. He stood up for what he believed in. When he spoke, others listened.

It was Ambrose who first stopped in his tracks at a vacant shop window on the bustling high street. A narrow retail unit nestled between a greengrocer and a shoe shop. Further along the street were now long-gone familiar names: Woolworths; Radio Rentals; Dixons; Freeman Hardy Willis.

He pressed his nose against the glass to look inside. There was evidence of an abandoned re-fit. Planks of wood leant stacked against the walls. Wires dangled from the ceiling. But being the visionary that he was, he could see what it could become.

'Let me describe it to you,' he said to me. I don't know whether the speech was rehearsed, but the manner in which he outlined the potential swept me up in his passion.

I only had one – albeit large – reservation. 'But neither of us know *how* to cut hair?'

'A minor detail,' he said. 'These things are

taught. There's nothing that can't be learnt.'

It was a prime example of refusing to let barriers get in the way. To focus on the goal.

Times, of course, were different then. We vowed never to forget that.

It was perfect, he insisted. We could be together every day, not having to conform. Did I really want to be a wage slave for somebody else's dream? Spend nine to five following the outdated rules of some narrow-minded despot? He was referring to my junior clerk position at the gas board. It was a job intended solely as a stop-gap measure, but which I knew caused him anxiety, afraid I might decide to climb the ladder there.

He didn't say it, but I knew too that the prospect would also enable him to continue with his activism. His true vocation. Calls to the switchboard were increasing and he was adamant that it was making a difference. But it needed more promotion and volunteers. He could not carry the load alone.

And so, a quick decision was made that would shape our entire lives. We enrolled on an evening crash course in basic barber skills and were relieved to discover that we both had a natural flair. This buoyed us as we spent the daytimes transforming the interior of the shop.

Ambrose, being both well-liked and well-connected, recalled favours from various contacts to assist with the more technical elements of the refurbishment. Wiring and plumbing were soon up to scratch. We got lucky too when word reached us of a fire sale at another barbershop that had closed due to the owner's ill-health. One of Ambrose's many mates had an old van in which we transported chairs, mirrors and even an old cash register.

There was a buzz. Passing shoppers watched as it rose like a phoenix, observing curiously the progress being made within. At the painting of the signage, *A & M Traditional Barbers*, passers-by began to ask when the shop would be open for business. And soon enough, a small crowd had gathered to applaud us cutting a ribbon at the door. At the time it had seemed like a grand gesture for such a little enterprise. But looking back, it was more than appropriate for the occasion.

Little had we known that our venture into the unknown would see us outlive so many of our retail contemporaries. The winds of change blew down that street. Our unflinching presence over the years entrenched us as stalwarts. A bastion of something familiar and constant in an ever-changing environment. Whilst fads and fashions changed, people always needed a haircut. We saw the demise of the greengrocer, the butcher, and the baker as supermarkets became established. Video stores and internet cafes appeared, boomed, and then vanished without a trace.

I don't know if Ambrose had foreseen it. But *A & M Traditional Barbers* achieved arguably as much as the activism. We became seen. We were known. And the community embraced us.

The premises had a simple layout. A small

room at its rear – practically a cupboard – served as a storage area and place to boil a kettle. In the shop itself, the cash register sat on a wooden counter. There was a coat stand and a display cabinet of grooming products for sale. A bench against one wall with a magazine rack on it served as a waiting area. We never took appointments. And in front of the mirrors and basins stood three chairs side by side.

Ambrose always worked at the one in the middle, and I at the one closest to the window.

The third chair provided opportunities for Ambrose's philanthropic nature by welcoming a constant flow of apprentices and work experience students. It did not matter what their backgrounds or experience were, all were encouraged to learn the ropes in order to build something better for themselves.

Ambrose took paternal pride in them. And in return, the majority kept in touch after their placements.

He was a father-figure and sage to many. Not just staff, but customers too.

For many, the twenty minutes in the chair was an opportunity not only to be heard but to seek advice and guidance. Ambrose approached his work in the same manner as the switchboard. He listened keenly to what others had to say and reflected their words back to them. He empathised.

I didn't consider us radical in any way. We were just being true to ourselves.

I suspect, in the early days, that most of the clientele considered us to be just good friends.

Maybe our togetherness had raised eyebrows. Who knows? Perhaps we had been the topic of conversations.

We knew first-hand the struggle. We lived it all. The dark times of ignorance and disease. The battles of inequality and prejudice. The highs of long fought for freedoms. All played out on stage in full view through the frame of a shop window.

Ambrose once told me that retaining a free-spirited nature was one of life's challenges. Not to be worn down by the lacerations of daily life but instead to be inquisitive – fascinated even – by everything we experience.

And so we approached everything in that way as a team.

It never crossed my mind that it was unusual to both live and work together. I suppose it wouldn't suit everybody. For some couples it would be their worst nightmare. But for us, it came as naturally as breathing. Having him always at my shoulder was a constant casual intimacy. He was always by my side.

We didn't say it, but I think we felt a responsibility. *A & M Traditional Barbers* was a constant fixture. And its owners represented something of a pioneering spirit. To even mention the possibility of moving on felt disloyal. So it was never discussed in front of, or with, the customers. We just let them assume that the status quo would continue indefinitely.

It was only at the end of the day, when the sign had been flipped to 'closed' that increasingly Ambrose had extolled the possibilities of retirement. He'd slump on to one of the chairs and kick his shoes off with a groan. Being on his feet all day had never troubled him before. But latterly it had exhausted him.

'What do you say to a sea-change, Munro?' he would say. 'How about swapping your view out of the window of the high street to one of the ocean?'

I leant on the broom handle. 'Ibiza?'

He'd laugh. Make jokes about toy boys and mankinis. Possibly developing an unhealthy drug habit.

'I'm thinking closer to home. Can't you see us kicking back on deckchairs?'

'Kiss-me-quick hats?'

'Knotted handkerchief for me,' he said, patting his head. 'And a string vest.'

The same conversation crept up most evenings. We quipped on the same ideas, lobbing back and forth fantasies of another life at the seaside. It served as a little escape.

We were testing the waters. I see that now. By making light of the situation we were gently nudging one another to see how far we could push it. Tentatively stretching the boundaries. With each time we spoke about it moving us an inch towards making a change.

But the groove we had carved over the years was a deep one.

I resumed sweeping the floor. I looked at the hair that had been gathered by the head of the broom.

'So when are we going to do it, Munro?' Ambrose asked. 'When are we going to shut up shop and move to Somerton-on-Sea?'

*

It was mid-morning on a Friday. One of those deep winter days when a thick cloud cover threatened to sleet and the daylight only just emerged from the long night to an insipid murk.

The bell above the door tinkled to a regular stream of customers.

Ambrose had embraced the Christmas spirit by donning a Santa hat and sang along to the classics being pumped out on the radio. I could always be sure of him to drape the place in tinsel and hang baubles from the mirrors. He loved the festive season. It was the sparkle, he said. It reminded him of being a boy and the importance of retaining some of that wonder.

In an attempt to entice the crowds, the traders had combined to fund a series of strung lights across the road. They flashed and glistened.

As I worked, I watched shoppers wrapped up snug in woolly hats and scarves pass by. Their breath lifted into the cold air as plumes of white vapour. They juggled bags and rolls of wrapping paper. The traffic was heavy and slow-moving. Fumes billowed from exhaust pipes.

There was condensation on the inside of the window. It gave the shop a dream-like quality. The atmosphere was jovial. Clippers buzzed and blades snipped. Conversations revolved around plans for the forthcoming holidays.

They were the moments to treasure - when it felt like a bubble. A bubble in which we felt safe and protected. Cosily ensconced in a universe of our own making. Cloaked in a warm blanket of contentedness. A soft release of endorphins. High and heady. Where the outside world – with all its fractious pace and frenzy – could not touch us.

There came, as there often did at that time of day, a lull.

Ambrose leant against his vacant chair. 'How about a mince pie with your morning coffee?'

My comb paused. The client in my chair was draped with a black plastic sheet around his neck. His hair was wet. I looked at him in the mirror. 'Where Ambrose is concerned,' I said, 'there is no such thing as *one* mince pie.'

The mood was light. Ambrose patted his belly.

'Don't you want to put a coat on?' I said as he opened the door to an icy blast. He was only in his shirt sleeves.

'You know I don't feel the cold.'

It was true. He never had.

I didn't even look at him. The supermarket was only a short walk. He would only be gone for five minutes. Maybe ten if there was a queue at the tills.

I heard the bell tinkle as the door closed.

I spoke with the man in the chair about something and nothing. Like so many conversations before the details would be forgotten. With a final blast from the hairdryer and an application of wax he was done and I was washing my hands in the basin. We continued to chit-chat. I thought nothing of the sound of a siren. We had become immune to them over the years.

As I dried my hands on a towel, I saw an old

woman in a camel coat with a little dog on a lead crossing the road. Her gaze was fixed on something further down the road. A blue light flashed in her eyes.

I took his payment in cash. As I slid the note into the till I looked up at the large antique clock on the wall.

He must have been held up. He was always bumping into people he knew.

I hoped he wasn't getting cold.

That's what I was thinking as a figure ran by the window and flung open the door with a crash. It was one of the regulars. He was flushed in the face and out of breath. He shook his head frantically.

'Munro,' he said. 'You need to come quick...'

10.

The guesthouse held its breath.

I placed my hand warily on the door handle. My mind had rattled through a lifetime of memories. I had been blind-sided again by the raw emotion of that winter's day. I felt flustered. In the mirror, I saw that my hair and clothes were dishevelled.

Calm down, I told myself. That's what you would have said if you were there. You always knew how to take the edge out of a difficult situation.

I steadied myself. The handle creaked as I turned it.

I opened the door cautiously, just an inch, to see who had knocked.

'Sorry to disturb you,' he said.

It was Wiktor.

I drew the door open fully.

'It's okay,' I said. 'You're not disturbing me.'

I caught a moment of concern in his eyes. He quickly looked me up and down. I felt embarrassed that he might have detected my flustered demeanour.

He, in comparison, looked solid and dependable. An ill-fitting orange T-shirt stretched over his wide mid-riff. Denim shorts and a sturdy pair of boots with chunky socks completed the look.

'You've been alone with your thoughts.'

The blue lights flashed in my head. I heard the siren.

I mumbled something incomprehensible.

I didn't know whether to invite him in. So instead, we hovered at the doorway.

'You remember Sandy?' he continued.

'Yes,' I replied, thinking of the stoop and the walking frame.

'He asked me to speak with you. Said it was important.'

'Me?' I said. 'Important?'

'Yes. He spoke to me when I put his socks on this morning. He said he has a *proposition* for you. Yes?'

Proposition must have been Sandy's word.

It was an interesting one.

'Oh,' was all I could muster.

'He hopes it is not too late...'

The scrap of paper on which Wiktor had written down the address flapped furiously in my hand. A breeze was whipping in from the east.

As I approached Marine View Court along the promenade, I looked at its striking design. It was an unusual building constructed out of brick with balconies rendered white along its frontage. Its length and height embodied somewhat of an ocean-liner vibe. It was of another era.

Gazing up at it, I noticed wisps of mist rolling gently over the brow of the cliffs. Filtered sunlight gave it an other-worldly evanescence. The weather in Somerton-on-Sea had certainly proved to be changeable.

I was baffled by Sandy's invitation to visit. A rostered shift at the café would prevent Wiktor from joining us, he'd told me. But Sandy would be grateful to see me at any time. 'Just be patient when you press door buzzer,' Wiktor said. 'He does not move quick. Sometimes he does not hear. And sometimes he's asleep. So just keep pressing the button.'

A small path lined with lavender led to gleaming double doors beneath a canopy. The whole place gave the impression of being immaculately maintained and cared for. On the right-hand side was a shiny brass plate of numbered buttons. I looked again at the scrawl and then pressed number twenty-two.

I self-consciously tapped my foot.

No reply.

What was I doing here? I wondered. I looked again at the tumbling mist. Was I wasting valuable time? Weren't there more pressing things I should be doing?

'Hello?'

I jumped. The crackly voice from the intercom had startled me.

'Hello. Sandy?' I shouted into the speaker.

'Yes?'

'It's Munro! We met on the seafront.'

'I'll buzz you in. I'm on the top floor. There's a lift.'

The double doors rattled and I heard a catch being released. I reached out and let myself in. I was greeted by a smart lobby of polished wood walls and tiled floor. A slim table against the wall had a vase of fresh blooms upon it.

There was a staircase, but I opted for the lift as instructed which rose me sedately up to the highest level. The doors contracted with a ping and I stepped into a corridor of numbered doors. The carpet felt plush beneath my shoes. I was intrigued by the place. And by what Sandy had to say.

The numbers on his door were glistening brass. I gave a quick rap on the knocker.

I heard him approach with short shuffled steps. I had not seen him long enough on our previous encounter to commit his features to memory, but on opening the door he was entirely recognisable and familiar to me. His watery eyes glinted as he smiled.

'Good to see you,' he said.

'A nice place you have here,' I said.

'You think so?'

I was genuine in my admiration. His home was surprisingly spacious and airy. And despite the descending sea mist, it was incredibly light.

He manoeuvred his walking frame and I followed his slow progress through the hallway. I sensed something deliberate in his pace. We passed a series of photos of motorbikes on the wall.

'Did you take these?' I asked.

'It was a hobby of mine,' he said in a dismissive way.

We moved into a wide open-plan lounge and dining room. From the windows and glass doors to the balcony was a spectacular vista of the sea which today was shrouded but on clear days, I imagined, must have stretched out for miles. I could barely take my eyes away from the view.

'What an amazing aspect,' I said.

'You think so?' He negotiated himself into a

wing-back chair. 'Take a seat,' he said, indicating a spot on a cream-coloured sofa. The neutral décor and natural tones of the room had an inviting feel. I wondered how much of its cleanliness was down to Wiktor. I could see no evidence of dust.

He offered me afternoon tea, but I declined. He wasn't offended. If anything, he looked relieved not to have to move again from his seat. 'I appreciate you coming to see me,' he said. 'I was hoping to share a story with you...'

'A story?'

'You might find it hard to believe, but I was young once.'

'We all were,' I said.

'Education didn't suit me. I couldn't see how books were going to help me and the lessons did not hold my attention. The rules made me feel like a caged animal. I was always getting into scrapes.'

'Fights?'

'Wouldn't think it of me now, eh?' He gave a wry smile. 'But in those days, I was wily and full of energy. I might have been small in stature, but I was strong and fierce in character.'

I thought of my own schooldays and wondered whether Sandy had been the type who had made my life a misery.

'You said you have always lived here. So you had family?'

'Yes. My parents had a volatile relationship. Dad was a builder. Liked a drink and to put money on the horses which often meant that things were tight at home.'

'Any siblings?'

'An older brother. We didn't get on. I think he always resented the attention I received as the younger son. He thought I was given more slack.' He straightened his posture in his chair. 'The only thing we really had in common were our attempts to protect Mum when Dad came home roaring drunk. If he'd had a loss on the horses, he could be relied on to be in a foul mood. But on some occasions, there was no apparent cause for his rage. It was just the booze.'

It was not, unfortunately, in my experience an uncommon tale. Over time, many men in the barbershop chair had confided similar stories. We never judged. It was their time to talk. And an opportunity to be heard.

'Was there violence?'

Sandy nodded. 'Dad was a boxer in his youth. He knew how to use his fists.'

'It sounds like a difficult environment to grow up in.'

'I'm not making excuses, but I don't think it helped my own behaviour. It gave me a rebellious streak. And on flunking school with no qualifications, I quickly discovered motorbikes and leathers. It wasn't just the freedom of the open road or the thrill of being a speed demon. It was the roaring sense of being part of a tribe.'

I had not put Sandy down as an ageing rocker. Only now, having been told could I see a distant twinkle in his eye.

He gazed into empty space. 'It was what went against me, I suppose,' he said.

'What do you mean?'

'Seaside towns are small places. Reputations go before you. Often you are known before you have even met. That can be a bitter pill to swallow as a young man. I was labelled a layabout rocker from a troubled family. And perhaps in some confused way I felt a need to live up to that perception.'

'Sounds like you were finding your feet,' I said. Easier, of course, to say that now.

'I already knew of your cousins, of course. Everybody did. They were in a younger year at school and were something of a curiosity. Always together. Always with the same hairstyle. Always side by side. It was like seeing double.'

The twins of my childhood sprung to life in my mind as vivid and real as they had ever been.

'It was a chance encounter. A little gelato place on the front. The bikes were lined up and gleaming outside. Our raucous mob swarmed the place, a mass of black jackets and helmets. The pair of them had been sitting at a table in the window. A mirror image. Except one looked at me more than the other. So we struck up a conversation.'

'Lana or Pearl?' I asked.

He laughed. 'That was always the joke. Two for the price of one! That's what the lads said.' His faraway look said to me that he spoke of those no longer with us. 'But I always knew the difference. Lana was the girl for me.'

I recalled Lana's mention of a boy and wondered whether this was one and the same thing.

'Do you believe in love at first sight?' he asked.

I thought of you. 'Yes. Yes, I do.'

'Then I don't need to explain. We were smitten with one another. She was the first girl to see the true me. She could see right through the tough guy image.'

'You courted?'

'That's an old-fashioned word. And yes, I suppose we did. But in a secretive way because Lana was always wary. I think she always knew.'

'Knew?' I said. 'Knew what?'

'That her parents would disapprove of me. Of *us*.' He looked troubled. 'I should've fought for her. But I didn't know how. Her father was a force to be reckoned with and he soon put a stop to it.'

The depiction of Uncle Graham was accurate. It was exactly as I thought of him.

'I heard what happened to her parents,' said Sandy. 'And I'm ashamed to say I almost felt pleased. As if justice had been served. But then I thought of Lana and how it must have been for her. And then I wasn't pleased at all.'

'You didn't approach her?'

'Time had passed. By that time, we were strangers. It wasn't for me to get involved. So I moved on. You have to, don't you? I married twice. Both unsuccessfully. No children.' The brevity of his life story was clinical. 'But I always held a candle for her. Perhaps that's why my relationships never lasted. Anyhow, it's just me now.'

His story appeared to be over. But why had he told me? I hoped he wasn't going to ask me to play cupid. Too late, I feared, for that.

'Do you think,' he asked, 'that we come to

87

regret the things we *don't* do more than the things we *do*?'

I thought of you. And Somerton-on-Sea.

'I don't know,' I said. Entirely honestly.

'Me neither. All I know for certain Munro, is that I'm tired of looking after myself. It's all too much for me. What I want, and it's not much to ask, is somebody to put food in front of me. I don't want to worry that if I fall over there'll be nobody around.' He had clearly been giving it some thought. 'There's a residential place in town. They promise to make you feel independent but there's help on hand round the clock. And there's a lounge with activities where you can get involved as much or as little as you like.'

The mist beyond the window had developed into a thick fog.

'All I need is for someone to buy this place,' he said. 'So Munro, what do you say?'

On my return, the guesthouse was almost invisible. Only its faint outline was visible through the fog.

I had lost track of time. In the absence of any of my usual daily routines I suddenly felt cast adrift. It made me think of those terrible first days after you'd gone. I had lost my rock and I floundered. Never knowing whether I would recover again.

I would chew over Sandy's offer. The flat wasn't at all what we'd have lived in.

I was in a spin.

The interior of the guesthouse felt cool. It must

have been the sound of the front door closing that prompted Lana to dart out into Reception.

Her face was pale and crumpled.

'What's wrong?' I asked.

'It's Pearl,' she said. 'She's missing...'

11.

The fog swirled around me. I wondered whether this is what it had felt like for you as you slipped away on that wintry Friday morning. A white cloud obscuring the landmarks. Disembodied sounds.

Had you drifted up through the clouds casually observing the drama unfolding beneath you?

You had collapsed outside Boots. A heart attack. It had been quick, they'd said, as if somehow that might have been a good thing. I suppose they meant for you.

By the time I got to you an ambulance was already on the scene. A crowd of curious onlookers had gathered. Elbows nudged with morbid intrigue. You lay on your back on the pavement. I was held back by medics as I attempted to explain who you were to me. Only able to watch their frantic attempts to revive you at a distance.

But there was nothing they could do. It was too late.

You were gone.

I have lost count of the number of times that scene has played in my mind. It creeps up on me. Pounces when I least expect it. And every time it is as real as the moment it happened. The emotions are as raw and brutal as they ever were. They have not faded. They are sharp and painful.

It will forever represent the before and after. A schism in time.

Life before was predictable. In a comforting

way. Like a favourite sweater. I wore it without thought and it sat easily upon me.

If it had ever crossed my mind that it wouldn't be like that forever, I don't remember.

Whereas now, everything feels unfamiliar to me. I see things with different eyes. As if everything is fragile and in danger of being broken.

I am disorientated. My surroundings are a whirl of things both past and present. I can hear car engines and seagulls above the sound of the sea. My weary body is only being carried on by a hit of adrenalin. Perhaps because of what happened to you, my instinct to leap into immediate action is strong.

'It's not the first time,' Lana said. 'She has started to wander.'

'Let's not panic.'

'But look at the weather!'

I suspected that Lana, like me, was scrolling through all the dangers that lay hidden in the fog: busy roads, cliff edges, even the railway line.

'She can't have gone far,' I said.

Lana looked doubtful.

'Do you think we should alert the police?' she said.

I didn't know. Was it an over-reaction? Lana, I felt, was better placed to judge the severity of the situation at hand.

As if sensing my hesitance, Lana said, 'It's not Pearl's fault. It's her condition. It's deteriorating. She's gone downhill so fast.'

She sounded almost apologetic which I didn't think was necessary.

'You say this has happened before?'

'Yes,' she said. 'A couple of times. She's just slipped out quickly and then not been able to find her way back home again.'

'How did you find her last time?'

'By chance. The landlord of The Anchor was clearing outside tables when he saw her on the street. He said she looked confused and was concerned. He knew us, of course. Everyone who lives in Somerton-on-Sea does.'

'And he alerted you?'

'Yes. He phoned me. Told me Pearl was safe with him. We were lucky. It was something of a wake-up call to me. I vowed to keep a closer eye on her. But I haven't succeeded.'

'Don't blame yourself,' I said. 'You're doing your best.'

I asked her to list the potential places Pearl may have headed to. Were there any old haunts that might attract her? Together we put them in order of likelihood, but I kept to myself a sinking feeling that I might struggle to find these places in the fog. It might be an impossible task. But I didn't say that.

Instead, we agreed that I should work through the list of possibilities on foot and Lana should stay at the guesthouse in case Pearl should return. And if she did so, Lana would call my phone to let me know. We decided that there was no harm in Lana calling the local police station for advice.

And so I found myself pacing through the zig-zagging streets calling out Pearl's name into the inclement weather. It made sense, in light of

Lana's story, to head in the general direction of The Anchor. I hoped that she would be wandering in that vicinity as she had before but if even for me the fog was disorientating, I had little faith that she would find her bearings. It was barely possible to see my raised hand before my face.

I reached what seemed to be a narrow crossroad. Only the sound of traffic and the downward sloping terrain indicated to me the direction of the seafront.

'Pearl?' I called, as if trying to attract the attention of a lost pet. 'Pearl?'

Stumbling alone in my search, my train of thought jumped about like a grasshopper. One moment I was thinking about the story Sandy had told about Lana. Had there really been a chance that they could have lived happily ever after? Or was it just another example of rose-tinted spectacles? And then my mind flipped again to my own situation. I thought of the Sold sign outside the house. I ran through the pros and cons of Sandy's offer. It had been made so abruptly that at first I couldn't process it. I had entered the apartment in the role of curious visitor not as a potential buyer. I hadn't really been *looking*. I thought of his photos on the wall. It was his possessions that I'd been taking in, trying to get to know more about him; his story, his character.

I tried to conjure it up in my imagination. I sketched a mental floorplan in my head, but it lacked detail. What size were the bedrooms? How were the kitchen and bathroom laid out? I couldn't be sure.

All I was left with was a residual *feeling* of which I found difficult to define.

A lorry roared by. I had reached a busier stretch of road.

I felt guilty that my mind had wandered from the job at hand.

'Pearl?' I shouted, but my voice was lost in the passing traffic. I was getting hoarse.

As I approached the outskirts of the town centre I remembered Pearl's observation at how Somerton-on-Sea had changed over the years. Even through my eyes, as a stranger, it seemed to have grown in size and pace.

This struck me as unusual. Wasn't it usually that places seemed smaller than how we remember them as children? More common to discover that places have shrunk rather than grown.

Before my visit, I could have sworn to the geography of the place. As a boy I had traipsed every nook and cranny during those summer holidays. I had seen myself as an explorer staking my claim, devouring it all with absolute freedom. So it was a surprise to discover that the streets did not connect the way I remembered. The homes did not look the same. Either my memory had proved to be unreliable, or my mind had played tricks on me.

I crossed the road and began to encounter other pedestrians. Had they, I asked, seen anyone of Pearl's description? No, they said sympathetically turning their heads back and forth in futile well-meaning gestures. It would be difficult to find anybody in this fog. And there are so many people about with the festival.

I wondered what the outcome of Lana's phone call to the police station had been. The enormity of searching for Pearl alone was growing apparent. I began to frantically enter shops and eateries along the way. I stumbled over my words and was impatient at any hint of disinterest or lack of concern in those I accosted.

On reaching The Anchor a slight breeze arose, and the pub sign became visible through the mist. The weather had deterred customers from occupying the wooden tables outside and my inert position proved unpopular with those trying to pass by. I was an obstacle in their way. The bodies squeezed around me in both directions. It was a jumble of shouted conversations and screaming children. There was no way I would spot Pearl in such a marauding throng.

Rather than remain an obstruction on the path I surrendered to the predominant flow of foot traffic and continued to hope for a sighting. It was only the suggestion that the fog was lifting that gave me some hope that I might find Pearl.

Where next?

I tried to put myself in Pearl's shoes. Was there any logic to her thoughts now? Would she head to somewhere significant or was she just lost? Better, I figured, to hope for the best. Too frightening to consider the possibility of the ring road or the train line.

A squally gust hit me.

I made my way on to the promenade where

there were less people. The beaches were occupied by only a few stragglers buffeted by the wind and the flurries of mist.

I wasn't sure I knew Pearl anymore. I had spent so little time with her. The only things I could surmise about her were based on our few stilted interactions. Her confusion with room bookings leapt to mind. Her frustration and aggression at the breakfast orders in the kitchen.

Those events gave no clue as to her whereabouts now.

I stopped abruptly. A miniscule idea was forming in my mind.

I darted to the railings and grabbed hold of them fiercely. Think, I told myself. Think. Think. Think. Don't let the idea slip away.

The watery panorama expanded before me. It stretched from west to east through the lifting fog.

I blocked out the machinations of the town carrying on regardless behind me.

That's when it came to me. The only time – the briefest of moments – when Pearl had appeared almost as I remembered her was during our meal at the dinner table. She had relaxed during our reminiscences about the times we had shared during my childhood holidays. It was a brief recollection she gave about us scrambling across the rocks in order to see the lighthouse beyond the curve of the ragged cliffs. We had made it there and back, she remembered, before the tide rolled back in.

I looked apprehensively in that direction.

With nothing else to go on I let go of the

railings and strode east along the promenade. The initial stretch was longer than anticipated. I was out of breath as I made my way down the steps to the furthest beach on which suddenly my steps were wobbly on pebbles and sand.

I was not really thinking now. My concentration was entirely focused on my uneven progress towards the location of Pearl's story.

The edge of the sea crashed in curls in the mid-distance. Was the tide approaching or in retreat?

It was foolhardy, but something of the boy I had once been spurred me on.

Beneath the soaring face of the cliffs the rocks became larger, dark grey boulders with edges worn smooth by the motion of the sea. I placed one foot precariously on the slippery surface and spread out my arms to try and help me balance. It was possible, in places, to steady myself by placing the palm of my hand against the looming wall of chalk. We had never stopped to consider the risk of rockfalls as children.

At the point at which the cliffs curved I paused momentarily to catch my breath. In moving forward, I knew that the obstruction would obscure any sight of me from the promenade. If I was wrong – which was highly likely – and if Pearl was not immediately visible, I vowed to retrace my steps immediately.

I edged towards the turn.

My ankles suddenly felt weak.

The red and white stripes of the lighthouse appeared just as Pearl had described. I couldn't help but wonder in awe how the ravages of time had not altered it a jot. It was only the waves crashing against its base that jolted me back into the moment. Had the sea drawn closer?

I pushed on forward despite my misgivings.

At first, I didn't see the figure ahead of me. Its silhouette blended into the surroundings. It was only with a second closer look that I saw her.

'Pearl?' I shouted through the splashes and the cries of gulls.

She stood entirely still. Only her white hair and the hem of her skirt showed any movement in the breeze.

I needed to get closer, but the next section before me looked even more hazardous than what had come before.

It was virtually on hands and knees that I managed to get within earshot of her.

'Pearl!' I shouted again. The murky water had moved in fast. It frothed and fizzed around us. 'Pearl!'

As the waves lapped furiously towards us, she turned and gazed at me with a broken look upon her face. I wondered whether she was aware of the changes within her. I remembered what she had said to me about letting the side down.

Until now, it hadn't occurred to me that she might have come to this spot for an awful reason.

I attempted to signal her towards me. My hands and knees slipped beneath me.

'Come this way,' I croaked. 'We need to get back to dry land!'

I reached out my hand and beckoned her.

I tried to raise myself up, but my foot gave way beneath me. She stared at me clinging pathetically to the rock, an exhausted bedraggled old fool.

'Daddy?' she said.

The ocean threatened to lap its heavy cloak around us. There was only one thing I hoped would budge her. It was the only thing left in my arsenal.

'Lana needs you,' I pleaded.

I outstretched my arm to her. And prayed that she would start to make her way towards me...

12.

Neither of us seemed capable of moving. Both of us frozen in our perilous positions. We gawped helplessly at one another.

Hope was fading fast. The water whirlpooled around us. It frothed and swirled, hissing up through cracks in the rocks. In places it was seeping across the surface in furious rivulets. With each ebb and flow the ocean grew ever nearer.

I detected a rising panic in Pearl's eyes. Her damp shoes had drawn her attention. I feared that she was thinking of her parents and the terrible fate they had endured.

For Pearl to do anything erratic now might be disastrous.

Determined not to be stranded, I told myself not to give up. I refused to accept that this could end anything other than happily. I must remain calm for Pearl's benefit even though my heart was pounding in my chest.

'Remember what we did in the past, Pearl?' I called. 'It's just a game!'

'Munro?' she said. A moment of lucidity.

'Yes! I'm here!'

'I'm frightened. The sea is too close.'

'Don't be,' I said. I thought of her account at the dinner table. 'We found our way back before. We just have to do the same thing again.'

A wave hit one of the boulders and shot a giant spray of water into the air. Pearl faltered. She stumbled but quickly gathered herself upright again.

'There's no time to think about it. Just make your way towards me.'

Apparently galvanised by the shock of almost being knocked off balance, she tentatively began to sidestep her way towards me.

'That's the way!'

I held my breath as she tip-toed closer across the seaweed and barnacles.

On almost reaching me, another more ferocious wave bore down upon us, cold and salty. She gave a cry as she lost her footing. But with a final lurch she hurled herself in my direction.

'Well done,' I said. We were soaked through. I grasped her slippery hand. 'Now let's get home together...'

We were to learn later that Lana's phone call to the police had been taken seriously. In such cases, they explained calmly to her, the first hours are critical in successfully locating the missing person. Lana, they said, had done the right thing. An alert would be radioed out to all patrols both in cars and on foot in the vicinity. Community Support Officers would conduct immediate enquiries as to any potential sightings of anybody resembling Pearl's description.

It was this quick response that resulted in a police car driving slowly along the promenade just when two sodden figures emerged from behind the curvature of the cliffs.

We clung to one another. It brought to mind a three-legged race.

Pearl's teeth chattered. Whether from the cold water or from shock I didn't know.

'Are you cross with me?' she stuttered.

'Don't be silly,' I said. 'No harm's been done.'

But it was as if she couldn't hear. And again she said, 'Are you cross with me? Are you angry?'

Then before I knew what was happening, two police officers were scrambling towards us. They wrapped their thick luminous jackets around our shoulders and aided us back across the beach. I was relieved. But my hackles rose slightly at the tone of their voices. They spoke loudly and slowly to us as if we were two doddery old dears.

Which, of course, we were.

My pride was dented. That was all. Embarrassing to think of oneself having to be rescued.

They ushered us into the backseat of the car which felt warm and safe. A message was relayed through a crackly radio. All parties found safe and sound. Being returned home now. Over.

'Have we done something wrong?' said Pearl.

'No, Pearl.' I reassured her. 'Nobody's done anything wrong.'

The scene that greeted us upon our return to the guesthouse was one of pandemonium. Having pulled their patrol car up at the front door, the officers ushered us into the Reception where a number of late check-ins were surrounded by their suitcases and jostling to be served. A frazzled Lana, who had previously been the one to restore order at the front desk, was hunched over the reservations book.

The addition of two dripping bodies accompanied by police uniforms did nothing to alleviate the chaos.

Lana stopped what she was doing and turned her attention upon us fully. One of the visitors continued to complain but she ignored him entirely. Instead, she lunged towards us with outstretched arms thanking me and the officers profusely for finding Pearl safely.

'Thank goodness you're safe,' she said to Pearl. 'Don't ever give me a fright like that again, you hear me? Promise?'

Pearl nodded. Her bottom lip trembled. Sadly, I wasn't sure it was a promise she would remember making.

'Let's get the kettle on,' said Lana gesturing for us to move through into their private quarters. She asked that the assembled waiting guests excuse us. 'The weather has improved now. So you might like to take a stroll.' She was sure they understood and thanked them for their patience. 'All in good time,' she said vaguely.

From the bedroom window, the increasingly familiar view of Somerton-on-Sea had a golden haze to it. The sea breeze of earlier had completely gone leaving the events of the day feeling unreal. Now, it was still. The gulls soared high in the pale blue sky.

An equilibrium had quickly been returned. The two officers hadn't stayed long. Other duties beckoned. But their brief presence revealed them to be more light-hearted and convivial than on first appearances. A front, I realised, was probably a prerequisite for the job. We even shared a few laughs as I thought how distinctly at odds their uniforms looked in the genteel quarters.

After their departure, Lana had ensconced Pearl in front of the television with a mug of sweet tea before retreating to the kitchen where I relayed to her what had happened.

'It was our talk of childhood holidays that put me on to her,' I said.

'You did well to think of it. A stroke of luck. I dread to think what might have happened if you hadn't had the idea.'

I saw the encroaching water in my mind's eye.

Lana clutched her mug. 'It's a wake-up call. For me, in particular. I had hoped that we might've been able to just carry on with the status quo, but that's just delaying the inevitable. I thought it was easier to avoid doing anything about it. But I can't keep my head buried in the sand any longer.'

It was too soon, I figured, to discuss the options. Though I could see that she had opened the door a sliver to the possibility of change. But not yet sure of what lay beyond.

I wasn't the only one facing choices.

I gazed out at the view. The white sails of a faraway yacht came into view, and I followed its progress across the seascape. There was always something to see here.

I thought of the large windows in Sandy's apartment.

The conversation with Lana had meandered somewhat inevitably to my own circumstances.

Was I, she asked, any closer to a decision?

I gave a highly edited account of the development in my property search. It had not felt like the right time to disclose who owned the place or its connections to Lana. Stories, I figured, have to be told in their own time. And now was not the time. Another day, perhaps.

'It sounds like you may have found what you are looking for,' she said.

'Maybe,' I replied. 'Maybe I have.'

As I made my way down the staircase, I wondered what you would have made of it all. I felt certain that you were encouraging me from the sidelines. You were always my biggest cheerleader.

The wooden stairs creaked.

I had made a decision.

I would stop counting the days since you had gone. It was as if you had spoken. Your voice was loud and clear. You didn't want that. Not for me. Not for us. We weren't a couple who only lived to look at things over our shoulders.

Ambrose was telling me to live in the present.

The present?

With each step down I tried to nail it. But all I could muster was somewhere blurry between past and future.

I took the time to look at my surroundings. I felt the smooth finish of the banister and looked at the intricate carved motifs on its spindles. The building emanated a strength, but I knew that its future hung in the balance. It too was contemplating what tomorrow might hold having had its owners face the tipping point I had witnessed.

A vivid memory of scampering up the stairs as a boy returned to me. I was calling down excitedly to my parents below who followed me in leisurely pursuit.

The staircase was empty now.

On reaching Reception I recalled how I'd felt about our own house. This space too had the feeling of an artificial unoccupied stage set. The players from the theatre company were absent. I thought of all the scenes that had been performed. The bell on the desk dared me to strike it mischievously, as I had in my youth, and bring the place to life. But I resisted.

I took a shortcut through the empty breakfast room where the French windows were propped open to the overgrown garden below. The vacant tables made me feel sentimental. It was as if nostalgia oozed from the walls.

At the peak of the flagstone steps, I paused for a moment to take in the glossy mass of foliage. It smelt both fresh and dank.

His location on a bench in the mottled shadows delayed my initial sighting of him. He was hunched over with head in hands.

I was considering whether to slink away unnoticed when he looked up with a blotchy face and saw me.

'Wiktor?' I spoke. As I approached, I saw that he was crying. His eyes were red. I took a seat beside him. 'What's wrong?'

'This is a nice place to think, don't you think?'

I looked at the wildness around us. We were of

similar minds. 'Yes,' I said.

'I have had sad news from home. It is my grandmother. She has died.'

'I'm so sorry.'

'We were close. I speak to her on the phone every day.'

He broke down into deep sobs.

I laid my hand on his big shoulder. The gesture didn't seem like enough. I could feel my own tears approaching.

I swallowed hard.

'She knew I didn't feel safe there. She said she understood. She told me to be true to myself. To build a good life.' He wiped the tears from his cheeks with the back of his hands. 'I promised I would visit. Said I would see her again soon.'

I was unsure of what to say. I thought of the hours at the barbershop standing at the chair. Better just to listen.

He shook his head. 'Now it is too late. She is gone.'

The grief was palpable; immediate and raw.

'I remember always what she said to me: Wiktor, you must follow your dreams.'

'I think she was right. She sounds like a wise woman.'

'Yes. She was. Ale za każde marzenie trzeba zapłacić.'

I looked at him for a translation.

'But perhaps,' he said, 'every dream has to be paid for.'

THE END

Printed in Great Britain
by Amazon